Newness & Wonder

ALEXIS LYNNE

Newness and Wonder

Cover art and layout by JD Smith Designs

Editing by Jakki Leatherberry

ISBN: 978-0-692-19769-1

Dedication

For Lance, Lawrence, Annabelle, Remy,
Logan & still to be named #5.

Thank you for making every holiday perfect.

Chapter One

Tara Crowley stepped out of her front door and into the morning sunshine that was beginning to trail over her front deck. She smiled as she leaned over the railing and breathed deeply. It was early September, and though the leaves on the trees surrounding the cottage she shared with her sisters were still green, the air smelled of fall. For many, spring was the season of hope and renewal, but for Tara, it was the beautiful golds and reds of autumn that filled her with a sense of newness and wonder.

This smell in the air signaled the advent of the holidays—four months of busyness and joy that would bring Sylvan Hills much needed tourist dollars as well as a sense of community that was at its strongest during this time. Soon, the shops in town would be filled with travelers from neighboring states coming to view the magnificent fall foliage and abundant wildlife of the Blue Ridge Mountains. Not long after, the streets would be reclaimed by locals bringing their kids downtown for trick-or-treating and then again for the holiday art crawl and Christmas tree lighting on the square. During all the activity, the mountains would turn into a glorious fire-colored display before surrendering to the lights of Christmas.

Newness and wonder. Tara breathed it in once again before pushing away from the railing and turning to pick up her backpack, wincing a little from the weight as she adjusted it behind her. Stepping lightly down the steps into the driveway, she headed toward the trees that hid a footpath down the hill. The neighbors each took turns mowing the tiny trail when needed, but since she moved in with her sisters five years ago, the path had become mostly dirt. Within minutes, Tara was down the mountain and heading toward downtown, where she would empty her backpack in the various shops that sold her artwork and handmade jewelry.

Tara would miss the convenience of living within walking distance to town, especially during the crowded tourist season, when parking spaces were hard to find. As she gently swung her backpack to the ground and pulled out the handle to roll it now that she was on a sidewalk, she smiled at the reason why. After years of saving money, as well as all her hopes and wishes, she had made an offer on the aging farmhouse that had once belonged to her grandparents—the place of all her happiest childhood memories.

Along with her older sister, Shelby, Tara moved in with her grandmother after her parents' ugly and volatile divorce. Once everything was settled, their father moved south to Charleston to take a part-time teaching position, which would finance his true aspiration of being a full-time beach bum. Their mother, Frances, took her divorce settlement with her to Europe, where she spent years redefining herself. When she returned, she was no longer the farmer's daughter with little education or class. She was sophisticated and worldly and immediately set her sights on the richest lawyer in town, Tom Jackson, recently widowed and set to become the next mayor. Though she had mixed feelings, for the easily manipulated Tom, Tara was glad to have gotten a new sister out of her mother's machinations.

Charlotte had been her and Shelby's close friend while growing up, and the three had only grown closer in adulthood. Charlotte's mother had fought a bitter battle with cancer, succumbing just before Frances swept back into town. The three girls bonded over their resentment of their parents, but their love for each other kept them from wallowing in the pain for too long.

Tara loved living with her sisters, but the pull of her grandparents' farm was too much to resist. Her roots had kept her in this small town, even when ambition called her to larger cities to sell her art in galleries rather than gift shops or to surround herself with people who understood the need to create. Instead, her desire to live the peaceful life of her grandparents, to feel a connection to the earth beneath her and the land and animals surrounding her, fueled her every creation and her every hope.

The rich scent of coffee hit her as she reached Main Street, causing a rumble to sound beneath her sweater. The small bakery and café down the street was already busy with morning commuters stopping to fill their travel mugs with the best coffee in town. Tara quickly decided that would be one of her stops as she approached a beautifully wreathed, locked shop door and knocked. Many moments later, she was greeted by a weathered smile and kind eyes the same shade of green as her father's, as well as her own.

"Good morning, my dear! You are out far too early this morning."

Margaret "Lady" Crowley Winters was the owner of It's by Nature and Tara's great aunt. She was in her early seventies and moved slower every year, but she still had all the vibrancy she had possessed when Tara was little. Her family had moved to the area from a small antebellum town in southern Georgia, and Lady had never completely succumbed to mountain life. She was classy and elegant and had somehow maintained her distinctive Southern drawl even when everyone around her had the sharper accents of the mountains. The old men in town loved her.

"It's not too early for you, Aunt Lady. I'd bet you've been here at least an hour."

Lady ran a hand over her bobbed silver hair and sighed. "You forget that I'm old, dear. I can't sleep past sunrise. I think it is written in the old-lady code."

Tara laughed and moved farther into the shop filled with beautiful art pieces from many local craftspeople, including herself. Lady catered to the higher-end shopper, those with second homes in the mountains and tourists who wished to take home souvenirs other than plastic keychains and cheap snow globes.

"You are going to have to change that wreath soon. Blue and green no longer fit the smell in the air."

"You won't think that around three o'clock when it's eighty-five degrees out there."

"And you wonder why I am up so early? Let me pretend it's fall for a few more hours."

Lady smiled and led Tara to the back, where she began unloading carefully wrapped packages of beaded necklaces, ceramic serving pieces, and Christmas ornaments that Lady would begin displaying next month. These were just samples. Her aunt would decide how many to order.

"Tara," Lady breathed out the word, and she gently picked up a handled platter, painted in varying shades of red and orange, for inspection. "This is some of your best work. You must have spent months on these."

"I have been working on the collection all year, as well as the necklaces, in between orders for paintings and prints."

"I recently heard Joe say that he can't keep your work on the walls."

Joe Greene owned the art gallery across the street that specialized in local paintings. Tara was one on his best sellers.

"I have more work for him, too, but I will need to bring it in my car later. Canvas is too hard to carry down the mountain."

Lady laughed and patted her hand. "I can only imagine the number of hours you have been spending in that studio of yours. Has the Muse hit you that hard?"

"Financial need has hit me that hard." She sighed and then smiled. "I made an offer on the farm. Shelby expects to hear from the owners today, but since mine was the only offer after six months of being on the market, she thinks they will accept." Her sister was a real estate agent and property manager at the largest agency in Sylvan Hills and was representing her in the sale.

Her aunt eyed her speculatively. "That place needs a lot of work, Tara."

"Yes, that's why I have tried to produce more pieces this year. Do you think they will sell?"

"If we get as much traffic as they are predicting, then you will sell out before then end of the year. But, Tara, even with that—"

"I know. It's a big project, and I am prepared to take an adjunct position at the college or even a waitressing job if I need to. Brandon has offered to help me, and I will have some savings left after I make the down payment. I can make it all work. I am determined."

"My grandson is very handy, but a lot of that work will be more than the two of you can handle alone."

Tara felt an unwanted burst of annoyance rise inside her. Shelby had made those arguments and more as she was writing up the offer. She took a moment to breathe and visualize the farm returned to its glory. That always fought off the doubt when it came.

"Whatever comes my way, I will handle it. I have waited too long for the farm to come back to the family. I will never understand why my mother was so quick to sell it or why the current owners never did anything with it."

"Your mother hated that farm and everything it stood for. She wanted more from life. That's why she latched on to your father, who had a few dollars in his pocket at the time."

Tara pushed down old hurts but allowed resentment to continue to fuel her determination. Her parents had a miserable marriage, and they were generous in spreading that misery around. Her only happy moments from those years came from time with her grandparents. Even after her grandfather died, the farm was her sanctuary. "I just wish, for once, that she had thought of Shelby and me. We were happy there."

Lady stepped closer and put a hand on her arm. "I know, but it might not be wise to let that be your motivation. We have precious few years on this earth, my dear. Don't spend so many of them in the past."

Fighting back the tears that threatened, she bent down and zipped up her backpack. "I'm trying to build a future. Do you know how many you want to order?"

"I'm sorry, Tara. I did not mean to upset you."

Tara shrugged, refusing to let her excitement be quelled by reality. "You didn't. I know not everybody understands why this means so much to me. I am determined, however, that we all will spend Christmas there and everything will be as perfect as when Grammy would put on all her displays."

Her aunt pulled her into a sweet, Halston-scented hug. "She was a wonderful woman, and she would be happy to know you are carrying on her traditions."

"Thank you, Aunt Lady. Will you let me know soon what you would like to order?"

"Of course. Before you go, let me caution you against one more thing. I know you need money for the house, but if what you create becomes all about what you can sell, then you might as well give it up and go work a nine-to-five. Sometimes your dreams cannot coincide, and you must choose. Your art is genuine and comes from deep inside you. Do not lose that."

"That's what makes buying the farm so perfect. My greatest inspiration has always come from there. I look forward to using everything my gram taught me to build the place back up. And hopefully, the old barn can serve as a bigger studio than I have now and maybe even double as a gallery. Possibilities abound, and I intend to explore every one of them."

She kissed her aunt goodbye and headed out the door, her lightened backpack rolling behind her, heading to her next stop. By the time it was emptied, Tara was in need of caffeine supplementation, opting for a hot pumpkin spice latte even though the temperature was creeping up, replacing the fall-scented air with a trace of humidity that would annoy her if she gave it any thought. Instead, she removed her hoodie and sat on a bench on the corner, where she could sip on her latte and imagine the leaves turning on all the trees surrounding the farm.

Tara had only begun when her phone chimed the familiar ringtone that signaled her sister's call. Her heart started beating fast as she pulled the phone from her pocket. With shaky hands, she pressed answer and placed the phone to her ear.

"Hey, Shelby."

"Hey, Sister, where are you?"

"Downtown. I just delivered samples to Aunt Lady and everyone else. What's going on? Have you heard from the owners?"

"Yeah, I just got off the phone with the listing agent." Shelby paused. "Tara, they rejected your offer."

"Oh." Her heart sank, but she refused to panic. "So we need to write up another offer? There's some room to negotiate, right?"

"No, sweetie. They didn't counter. They rejected it outright. Another buyer made an offer a couple of days ago, and they accepted it. I'm so sorry."

Tara swallowed hard as a large knot formed in her stomach. "It's been on the market for six months with nothing happening, but in a week, they get two offers! Get them back on the phone, Shelby. I can go higher. I'll just need to take a teaching job."

"You can't beat this offer, Tara." Shelby named a figure that made her head spin. "They are taking the place as is and paying cash. The deal is going through. There's nothing we can do."

This was unbelievable. She put a hand over her mouth to stop the sob in the back of her throat from escaping. "No one around here has that kind of money."

"No. The buyer is from out of town."

"Great. More strangers coming in, only to lose interest when they see what work is involved."

"Maybe. Hopefully not. If they are willing to pay that much, then maybe they have plans for the place."

"Yeah. Maybe."

"I really am sorry, Tara. I wish there was something I could do."

Tara sniffed. "Me too."

"I'll come home early today. We'll open some wine, and I'll make lasagna for dinner. We can hate this guy and send bad mojo his way all night."

"Yeah, okay. I gotta go, Shelby."

She hung up before her sister could reply. She knew she should move and not sit crying on a bench on the corner like a sad fool, but she couldn't make her feet work. Once again, the home she always wanted was torn from her reach, and just like a decade earlier when her mother had first sold it out from under her, she was powerless to stop it.

Chapter Two

"Are you sure about this, Justin? It is an awfully long way to go."

Justin Hunter looked up from his suitcase, giving his cousin a sly smile before moving to his dresser to remove more clothes.

"Sylvan Hills is not another country, Annie. Just a couple hours by plane and then a short drive."

"Still, neither you nor Marley have ever lived anywhere else."

"And that's one of the many reasons we are making this move. I have to get her out of this city, Annie. Maybe in a smaller place she won't look so lost."

Marley, the twelve-year-old sister he barely knew, had come to live with him eight months prior after her actress mother died in a car accident. Their father, who had never been present in her life and far too present in Justin's, died from a heart attack a few years earlier.

"But she *is* lost, Justin. Are you sure moving her away from everything she has ever known is the right thing to do?"

Justin sighed and looked down at Ann, who had been his best friend as long as he could remember. Except for a short time after a car accident had severed her spine, causing paralysis in her lower body and driving her into a self-imposed isolation, they had always been inseparable. Their shared childhood experience of emotionally distant yet controlling fathers had bonded them, and now he would be moving away from the few family members he could tolerate.

"I remember the only times I felt anything other than grief and guilt after *my* mother died was when I was out of the city, where I had space to run free or yell into the wind or just think without sirens sounding all around. You, of all people, should realize that."

"I was twenty when I had my accident, and you were nineteen when your mother died. Marley is only twelve, and do I need to remind you that she barely knows you?"

Justin ran a hand through his thick, dark blond hair and sighed heavily. "Maybe I need space to sort through my guilt, too."

Ann titled her head and studied him for a moment. "You're her brother, not her father. You have not been responsible for her all these years."

"I should have been. No one knows better than me what a bastard our father was. Marley's mother barely had means to support them. It was one thing to cut me out of his will, but he did not provide for them at all as far as I could tell. Sharon was his mistress and Marley the biproduct. The most I ever did was send her a Christmas present every year."

"You were very young, still, and had just buried your mother when you found out about them. If a fifty-something man wasn't taking responsibility, what was a college kid supposed to do?"

"I haven't been a kid for some time now, Annie. You will not absolve me of this one. My determination to be nothing like him did not extend far enough. But I *will* take care of Marley now."

Ann sighed, seeming to give up the point for now. "Okay, so let's talk about this extreme behavior of yours."

He looked at her in amusement. "Extreme?"

"Yes! Marley's counselor suggested she get a pet or grow a garden, and you bought a farm. I call that extreme!"

Justin just stared at her, and eventually, she sighed, hopefully in resignation. He was determined that this move was best for both him and his sister but hated trying to explain all the reasons why. If he completely understood them himself, it might be easier.

"Just how small is this town you're moving to?"

"About three thousand people. The area is situated in a valley surrounded by hills and is greener than anything I've ever seen in my life. Do you realize you look just like your mother when you sneer like that?"

Justin could not help but laugh when the sneer became a scowl.

"Okay, so you are giving up everything—your job, your friends—to go play farmer. How are you ever going to find a wife in a town of three thousand people?"

He laughed, relieved that she was now teasing him. "Now you really do sound like your mother. And you know as well as I do that the job has been part of the problem. There's no way I could maintain those hours and give Marley the attention she needs. I've always hated it and, honestly, only became a lawyer to join a rival firm just to spite my old man. I just don't have the killer instinct you do."

Ann smiled proudly. "No, you don't. You are the black sheep of the family, the one with morals and a sense of obligation to the world."

"Like you don't."

"I'm better at hiding it than you are. I'm sorry if I sound unsupportive. I actually admire what you are willing to do to give your sister a better life. I'm just going to miss having my best friend close by, especially now."

"Why especially now?" She did not answer right away, which alarmed him. He returned to the bed and looked at her. "Annie?"

She smiled, and the knot in his stomach relaxed a little.

"While you are off digging in the dirt, I'll be growing a different sort of variety."

"You're pregnant?" The concern he was trying

to keep to himself must have shown because his cousin reached over and touched his arm.

"There is absolutely no reason why I cannot have a perfectly normal, healthy pregnancy. I've done all the research, talked to all the right people, and have all the best doctors."

Justin knew she would be getting it from all sides, knowing that both her husband, another high- powered attorney in their firm, and her mother would dote on her so much she would go nuts. He decided not to add his own concerns into the mix. Annie could handle herself and anything life handed her just fine.

"Yeah, but you're clumsy on a good day. How the hell are you going to manage with a big, round stomach? You're going to take a corner too fast and end up tipping over. I can see you on your back like a turtle waiting for someone to tip you back up."

Ann pinched him hard. "See. I need you to help keep me from going insane. Garret is already in full protector mode…and my mother!"

"I can imagine. Has she offered to move in with you yet?"

The pained look on her face told him yes.

"They both want me to quit the firm. They think it is too high stress and not good for the baby."

"And what do you think?"

"I think it's ridiculous. Women, even the *special* ones, do manage pregnancy and careers. Still, I have always planned to stay home once we started a family. I might talk a big game, Justin, but this is brand new territory for me. I can't help but be a little nervous."

"No one knows what's best for you better than you do. Follow your gut. It's never led you wrong."

"Is that what you are doing now? Following your gut?"

Justin nodded. "You are going to make fun of me, no doubt, but when I flew down to look at the place, it just felt right. It needs a lot of work, but I think it will be good for Marley to help with the repairs. I hope she will feel part of something larger, that there is more to the world than grief and anger."

"And who is going to help *you* with the repairs, Mr. Never Get My Hands Dirty Attorney?"

"Do I have to remind you that although my father was the never-get-his-hands-dirty type, but my mother's family were builders? I paid attention during my summer jobs on their sites, so I won't be completely helpless."

"They built skyscrapers, not barns, and they never lived far outside of the city either."

"Like I said, it's time for something new."

Finally, Ann's shoulders slumped, and she picked up a shirt to fold and place in his suitcase. "I guess there's nothing left to talk about. Let's get you packed and out of the city, Famer Brown."

Chapter Three

"Well, kiddo, what do you think?"

Marley looked up from her phone as if she just realized they had stopped. Pulling out her earbuds, she looked at him and then the house and snorted.

"You've got to be kidding."

Justin was so relieved not to be stepping into silence that he ignored the snide tone.

"Nope. This is our new home—all two thousand square feet and eighteen acres. Plenty of room to move and spread out."

"Definitely not the city. Probably can't even get decent takeout."

"Probably not, and when I was here looking at the place, cell reception was pretty spotty. I guess we'll have to learn how to cook and talk to each other."

The horrified look on her face was harder to ignore.

"Come on. Imagine the possibilities. Some paint. Some hard labor. A little love and care is all it needs, and then it will be ours forever."

"Isn't that what they say about strays?"

Justin laughed. "Well, I suppose you and I are the strays in this situation. You have three bedrooms to choose from. Wanna go check them out?"

She shrugged and got out of the car, carefully walking up the steps as if they might give way any moment. She was right to be cautious. The old farmhouse had not been cared for in the last few years and was clearly showing its age. But the bones were good. He had made sure of that before he purchased the place. He had no idea what he would do with all the land, but he had time to consider his options. The privilege of wealth was choice. His wealth had come with a hard price. Sometimes he wished for fewer options.

Carefully sliding from the car, he stretched his muscles, stiff from hours behind the wheel. He was tempted to follow behind his sister but remembered her counselor's words about giving her space to explore her own feelings. He would give her the chance to form her own opinion of the place before he insisted on pushing his.

When he decided to start fresh, he meant it, so all they had brought with them were clothes and a few sentimental items. He unloaded the suitcases and few boxes onto the porch and then allowed his anxiousness over Marley to get the best of him and made his way up the stairs to the bedrooms. The master was on the first floor, and three additional bedrooms were upstairs.

He did not find her in any of them, however, so he called out to her.

"I'm up here."

He turned to see a set of pull-down stairs just down the hall. Assuming they led to an attic of some sort, he carefully walked up them. The space seemed to run nearly the entire width of the house, with slanted ceilings and two small windows in the far wall. A few boxes were stacked in a corner with an old wooden easel propped against them.

"The former owners must have left some stuff. I'll call the realtor and ask her how to get it to them."

"I want this to be my room."

He turned to her in surprise. "This is an attic, Marley. It's meant for storage, not for living in."

"You said we were going to make this into a home. Why can't we turn this into a bedroom?"

Justin had to hunch slightly as he walked around. Some of the beams were low, but since Marley was unlikely to reach his six-foot-plus height, she wouldn't be banging her head in the years to come. It was an interesting space. He could see why a kid would want to hang out up there.

"We'd have to put in a real staircase and better floors. You wouldn't have a bathroom up here."

She just shrugged and continued to look around, as if imagining how it would look. Justin was pleased but still a little apprehensive. There would be an entire floor between them. The feeling that she wanted it that way bothered him.

"Well, are you going to let this be my room or not?"

"Yes, but you'll have to sleep in one of the other bedrooms until some work is done up here. Go on down and decide which one, and then we'll go into town to do some shopping and have dinner."

Marley walked passed him without saying anything, but he could see the gratitude in her features. That small smile made him feel like the best brother on the planet, and though he knew it wasn't likely to last long, he reveled in it.

A cloud passed in the sky, darkening the room further. Justin walked to the far side of the space, studying the two small windows there. The room would definitely need more light, perhaps with one large window instead of the two small ones providing some of it. He had to lean over slightly to look out, but the view from that angle was quite stunning. A large pasture spread out in between the back of the house and the base of a tree-covered mountain. The dark green leaves were starting to give way to the season with patches of red and gold beginning to spread throughout. Marley would have the best view in the house.

He smiled and pulled out his phone, texting the builder he had researched and spoken to just before the move. He wanted to get estimates right away so he could give his sister the room she wanted, hopefully by Christmas if not sooner. He felt good. This was the right place for them. How could it be wrong when it was so lovely. The thought had barely registered when the light flickered and went out.

* * *

The sound of a cork popping from a bottle reached Tara's ears, and despite the current fog clouding her mind, she readily looked up to see her smiling sister holding a bottle of wine.

"I thought this might get your attention." Shelby set three large glasses down on the coffee table and began pouring. "It's been weeks, sweetie. You can't keep moping about this. It isn't in your nature. It's over. The new owner has probably moved in by now."

Tara took a large drink and then looked into her glass. "He has. I saw a car in the driveway yesterday."

"Tara, please don't become some creepy stalker."

She sat up straighter and narrowed her eyes. "What do you mean? I just happened to be out that way."

Shelby sat down beside her and curled her legs beneath her.

"*That way* is nothing but land and a long stretch of road. You had no reason to be out there except to spy, little sister."

Tara said nothing, just grimaced and took another drink.

"Well, what all did you see?"

"Nothing, just a car and a few boxes on the porch. He must have just gotten there. I hate the idea of some hipster coming in and turning our family's farm into some upscale lemonade stand or something equally stupid."

"You don't know that's what he's going to do. You know nothing at all about the man."

"You're right. All I know is he stole the only thing I ever wanted."

"Then maybe it's time to want something else." Tara and Shelby turned to see Charlotte coming into the room, carrying her laptop and wearing a scowl that nearly matched Tara's. "Oh good, there's wine. Seriously, Tara, think about something else. *Do* something else. Paint something other than views from different places on the farm. Anything except this determination to be miserable."

Shelby reached over to give Tara's arm a gentle squeeze that matched her sympathetic gaze. Charlotte plopped down beside her, taking the last wine glass off the table and replacing it with her computer. Tara was stuck between nurturer and pragmatist when what she really wanted was someone to spew anger and bitterness right along with her. Considering she had no desire to see her mother just then, she poured more wine.

"Why do you have your laptop with you? Are

you writing?" Tara winced inwardly. Her step-sister had hidden behind her job as a freelance editor and virtual assistant for indie authors for years instead of working on her own book. She was a confident woman in all aspects of her life, except her writing, and she had been stuck on the same page for months. Apparently, Tara could spew viciousness without her mother's help. Charlotte, however, was classy enough not to take the bait.

"Get another bottle of wine, ladies. Actually, coffee might be the better choice. One of my clients has joined the video podcasting trend."

"Don't you encourage your clients to take advantage of new practices?" Shelby asked as she walked to the kitchen for another bottle.

"Yes, I do, but if she had mentioned this to me first, I would have advised her against it. You've heard of a face meant for radio? Well, this woman has a personality meant for paper."

Tara laughed, honestly laughed, for the first time in weeks, and tension eased from her and from the room. Part of her knew she had been making everyone around her miserable, but she just wasn't quite ready to move on. Dreams are not always so easy to let go of.

Charlotte opened her laptop. "Okay, girls, please tell me this isn't as bad as I am making it out to be. This is her third one, and she has just now asked me for feedback."

They watched as a washed-out, flat-voiced author spoke about—something. It was hard to tell with all the long pauses, random rants, and overall monotony of both her appearance and voice. There was one brief break from the flatness of it all when she turned her head and, honest to god, burped, loudly, during a live broadcast.

Charlotte covered her face with her hands and let out a soft sigh. "I'm going to lose another client."

"She asked you for your feedback, so surely she wants to improve. She won't fire you."

Tara wasn't so sure, and the look on Char's face said she agreed.

"She already fired me once for telling her the truth. I edited one book for her—well, half a book. I sent her an honest critique, which is what she asked for, and I didn't hear back from her for weeks. When I finally did, she told me that she had found friends to edit for her and that, in the future, she would only need me for marketing. When I tell her the truth this time, she's going to decide she doesn't need me at all."

"So she really doesn't want to improve. She just wants to do whatever she wants and magically have people like it. That's not art. That's a hobby. You shouldn't want to work with someone like that."

"I don't, but I do want to pay the bills. Anyway, that particular paycheck is a good as gone. You guys will foot the liquor purchases, won't you?"

Tara set down her glass and wrapped her arms around her sister, proud that Charlotte would not compromise truth just to get paid. If she ever found the courage to continue her own writing, Tara knew her sister would never produce anything that wasn't honest, just as art should be.

"Absolutely. I have a down payment that isn't going to be used. I might as well spend it on hooch."

"Now that's a much better attitude." Shelby returned her attention to the screen. "Do y'all remember when the radio station used to get people from the retirement home to come to the studio and read from the newspaper? There was that one woman who kept mispronouncing Beyoncé, and we had to turn it off because it was just too uncomfortable to see how out of touch she was. I think I prefer her to this."

Charlotte groaned. "It's actually a great idea, and I respect her for trying something new, but if we have this reaction, most of her readers will, too."

"Tell her that. Surely she doesn't want to look bad in front of her readers." Shelby was always the one who could see the bright side of everybody else's problems.

Charlotte snorted. "I guarantee you that if she thought it would sell books, she'd do ten of these a day. She's always been about marketing more than words. I suggested once that she start a book club for her readers. She said she didn't have time to read."

"But she's a writer. That's like me not going

to museums or other artists' studios. An artist gets inspiration from art. I don't like this person very much. Don't work with her anymore."

Tara was happy to have a new object of derision. She would likely be more sympathetic if she were sober, but for now, she would dislike this stranger with all the power of her own disappointment behind her.

Charlotte closed the laptop and sat back against the couch. "Bottom line, she does sell books. She's not a best seller, but what she does is good enough for her. If her readers are happy, then what I think doesn't matter."

Those were lovely and true words, but Tara knew it went deeper than that. When you care so much for something, it is hard to be around people who don't. Losing the farm hurt, but seeing the new owner neglecting such a gift would be worse. She finished her wine and closed her eyes, trying to find some vision that would bring her peace.

Chapter Four

Inhaling the strong, delicious scent of the coffee he just purchased, Justin sat down on a bench on the corner of Main and some other side street and watched the cars go by. Traffic was light. Most of the downtown shops had not yet opened, and he figured, by this time, most people were already at work or, like him, had dropped off their kids at school.

His coffee rested in one hand as he draped his arms on the back of the bench. The cool morning air ruffled his hair and helped calm his nerves after what was quickly becoming a typical hellish morning with Marley. That morning's argument centered around black lipstick and the ever-present phone glued to her hand. He hated the tension between them, but at least when she was yelling at him, she was not silent with her eyes focused on the screen.

He shoved down the niggling feeling that he was in over his head and reminded himself, again, that it would take time. The doubt inside him rose enough to whisper that it had been months since Marley came to him. How much more time would they need? It was a slight thought, but enough to make his stomach clinch and allow the fear of failing to wash over him. This was not a court case he could appeal after a loss. This was a life, his sister's life, and failure was not an option.

The sound of bells tinkling a few doors down distracted him from his dark thoughts. He turned toward the sound to see that a door had been propped open. Taking that as an invitation, he rose and took one last drink of coffee before depositing the cup in the trash and making his way toward the shop.

As he entered, soft music reached his ears only a moment before he registered familiar, woodsy smells with a touch of something softer mixed in, floral, he supposed. It was comforting and interesting at the same time, as was the eclectic mix of art and pottery pieces he saw as he looked around. This, he figured, was far more authentic than what he saw just a few doors down in the windows of the large General Store. This shop did not cater to the bargain hunters, but to those with a genuine desire to experience the beauty of the area, either in creating or taking the artwork home to enjoy.

The work surrounding him would not spend years in a junk drawer or on a dusty shelf. It would be valued. He smiled slightly in appreciation, and when he looked up to see a pair of green eyes focused on him, that appreciation switched from something artistic to something completely male.

The petite woman made her way around the counter, and his appreciation grew as the dark chocolate-colored waves draping over her shoulders bounced with each step. Those waves did not come from an expensive blow-out but were wild and natural. Then she smiled. The attraction was unexpected, but as a distraction from the dark thoughts of just a few minutes earlier, it would do nicely.

"Good morning. Can I help you with anything?"

The lack of smoothness that had made him such a terrible litigator surfaced, and in spite of his desire to say something witty and brilliant to the beautiful woman in front of him, he merely muttered a bland, "No, thanks, I'm just looking."

"Okay, well, if you need anything, I'll just be over there."

Justin nodded and cursed himself as she walked away. He wasn't a shy fifteen-year-old, and though he was hardly a Casanova, he had enough experience to know how to talk to a pretty girl. He shook off his disappointment and walked over to a display of beaded jewelry. What was he doing thinking about women anyway? He couldn't even handle the pint-sized version he was living with. That didn't stop him from looking back a time or two at the beautiful woman behind the counter or make his heart beat slower when he caught another glimpse of her warm, green eyes, but he eventually forced his attention to the display in front of him.

Thoughts of Marley took over as he traced a bracelet with his finger. Maybe a gift would help ease the tension. He'd seen her wear jewelry, and Ann had picked out a bead-making kit for him to give Marley one year for Christmas. Like every other decision that should be small concerning his sister, buying a simple beaded bracelet suddenly became far too complicated. He looked back to the shop girl, and though he would rather not give her more room to affect him the way she did, he asked her for help.

She smiled again and walked over in a completely normal, non-seductive way, and still, his throat went dry.

"I'd like to get something for my sister, but I'm not sure of her tastes. Do you know if twelve-year-old girls wear things like this?"

She looked at him appraisingly. "You have a twelve-year-old sister? That's quite an age difference."

"You mean I don't look eighteen? I'm not sure how to take that."

She smiled as her cheeks turned a slight pink, and seeing that small bit of embarrassment helped ease his own.

"Well, considering many eighteen-year-old boys would not take such care in choosing a gift for a little sister nor show such good taste in doing so, you should take it as a compliment."

He smiled broadly, enjoying the sound of her

voice and her light teasing. "Okay, you saved the sale."

"Whew. We're coming off the slow season, and I could use the money."

"Is this your shop?"

"No, it's my great aunt's. She had an appointment this morning, and I'm filling in. Those are my pieces, though."

He looked down at the jewelry display. "You made these?"

"I did, along with some of the pottery you see over there and the note cards and magnets by the register are print versions of my paintings."

Justin was impressed, and not just by her compact curves and enticing smile. Her eyes were soft and warm, and she had an obvious talent for creating beauty from something as simple as clay. "You're rather versatile. And quite talented from what I can see. Are these hand painted? It must take forever."

"It is time consuming, but the beads are larger when I paint them. I shrink them as part of the process."

"What is the significance of the design here?" Something told him she did not paint randomly, and he noticed earlier that most of the pieces had different designs.

She leaned in slightly, and he could smell the scent of her shampoo as she pointed to the bracelet in his hand. He swallowed and attempted to focus on what she was saying rather than how delicious she smelled or his desire to see if those waves felt as silky as they looked.

"The four beads on this one represent each season. You see the mountains here starting to green up in the spring."

"Green up?"

"Yes, that's what we locals say. We even have a Greening up the Mountains Festival. Spring comes to the valley first and then makes its way up the mountains. We watch as the green travels upwards, hence 'greening up.'"

"Ah. And the rest?"

"In summer, the rhododendrons bloom, making the hiking trails hard to resist. Fall, as you will soon see, is vibrant when the trees turn. People drive in from all over to see the changing colors. And in winter, after all the leaves have fallen and the Christmas displays have been put away, you can see houses dotting the mountains, reminding us that we have neighbors, though they and their houses are not always remembered during the rest of the year."

Her words charmed him, and her obvious passion for the area calmed his doubts. There was much to look forward to, and he and Marley would thrive here. Something in this woman's eyes told him so.

"Have you always lived here?"

"Pretty much. I went to art school in Georgia and worked at some museums and galleries on the coast for a while, but otherwise, this has always been my home."

He studied her for a moment and then realized he was completely captivated by this woman, and he didn't ever know her name. He put out his hand, and thankfully, she accepted the invitation.

"I'm Justin. I just moved here, and hearing you speak about the town makes me truly glad I did."

"I'm Tara. You'll have to tell my stepfather, the mayor, that. Perhaps he'll put me on the payroll."

"He could do worse things, I'm sure. Will you tell me more?"

She raised her eyebrows in question and then glanced down at their still-joined hands. He reluctantly let go of her hand. Still holding the bracelet, he gestured toward the register. "Tell me about the scenes you paint."

She nodded and walked to the display of notecards, picking up a stack tied with ribbon. She gently loosened the tie and spread each design on the counter. The cards were representations of watercolors and were as detailed and lovely as her jewelry. He wasn't surprised. Artists often put pieces of themselves in their work, and she was the loveliest thing he had encountered in a long time.

"Again, we have scenes of each season, from here in town and the surrounding areas. This is the train depot in Bryson City decorated for Christmas. This is our own courthouse with lighted trees on the lawn. This is the river in summer and more of the rhododendrons. Here is our downtown during the Greening Up Festival and one of my favorite views from childhood as the flowers are beginning to bloom. And fall is shown in two different views that I am fortunate enough to see from my own deck. One as the leaves are starting to turn and one where they have fallen enough that you can see downtown."

"Fortunate indeed. I'm getting the impression that fall is your favorite season."

"It beasts out Christmas only slightly."

"I look forward to seeing it in its glory. I'll take the bracelet and two packs of notecards. I have an aunt who still likes to send handwritten notes."

"No one writes letters anymore. It's nice to know these will see actual words written on them."

He watched as she rang up the sale and then carefully wrapped his items, thoughtfully placing the bracelet in a nice gift bag. He wanted to ask her to dinner and nearly blurted out the words before he remembered that there was no one to watch his sister, and he was not comfortable leaving her alone. Still, in spite of the very big reason he should not be getting involved with anyone, he did not want his time with her to be merely cursory. The passion she showed for the things she loved was addictive.

"I planned to spend the morning touring my new town. Will you get a lunch break?"

She hesitated for a moment and then folded her hands on the counter. Her response suddenly became the most important thing in the world.

"I don't know when my aunt will be back. I was planning on ordering in for lunch, but I wouldn't be opposed to having company."

He smiled in relief. "What's your favorite downtown restaurant?"

"Proud Larry's. Everything on the menu is good."

"Then I'll pick up lunch and see you around noon?"

She nodded and smiled softly. He reached out once again, taking her small hand in his. "It was lovely meeting you, Tara. I'll see you in a few hours."

"Enjoy your tour, Justin. Be warned, though, that you will fall in love quickly."

He smiled and walked from the shop, fearing her words were indeed true.

Chapter Five

Tara bit her lip and turned to stack the notecards and replace the ribbon. She had woken with a killer hangover that even her walk to downtown had not completely cleared. The sight of the tall, blond stranger, however, did what all the wine the night before had not—momentarily make her feel like something other than the bitter hag Charlotte had rightly accused her of being. Though no handsome face could erase her disappointment, the distraction of flirting with someone so clearly interested was impossible to resist.

Clamping down the urge to sigh like a giddy teenager, she tried to concentrate on reorganizing some of the displays, but her mind kept wondering back to Justin. Tara couldn't remember when she had been so instantly attracted to someone. Those gorgeous amber eyes and broad chest of his drew her attention as soon as he walked through the door. She wanted to sketch him, capture all that masculine appeal on paper, and she hadn't been interested in drawing anything but nature since her first nude experience at art school.

A man with that much appeal could easily be a player, but Tara had not gotten that vibe from him. He seemed like a nice guy by the way he cared about getting something for his sister and having ever noticed that his aunt sent handwritten notes. He also appreciated her work, which showed incredible taste and class. He had not said where he moved from. She could not detect an accent. That was one of the things she could ask when he came back.

She smiled as she had the brief thought that she was glad she met the newcomer before Shelby or Charlotte had spotted him. Her sisters were as different as night and day, but one thing they had in common was the ability to attract men. They loved Shelby's gentle beauty and Charlotte's more exotic looks and intensity. So far, though, no man had been good enough to catch their attention for long, though many tried.

"Is that display causing you any specific grief, or do you have a hangover?"

Tara turned to see her cousin Brandon towering over her, wearing a frown that made her wonder if he had had his own night of overindulgence.

"What makes you think I have a hangover?"

"Because I just saw Charlotte, and she had the same look. It usually means y'all tied one on."

Ah. The scowl was explained. Brandon was one of those men who had not been deemed good enough, though, bless him, he had never given up. He fell hard for Charlotte in high school, years before she became Tara's stepsister. Though Brandon was one of the best guys around, Charlotte just never could picture them together. It made Tara sad for Brandon, but the guy had to give up eventually.

"Where did you see Charlotte?"

"In the coffee shop—with some guy. A tourist by the looks of him."

"Oh." Tara's heart sank. "What did he look like?"

"I don't know. Short."

"Everyone seems short to you, Paul Bunyan. What color hair did he have?"

"Brown, why?"

Relieved, Tara just shrugged. "If you're looking for your grandmother, she's not here. She had a doctor's appointment this morning."

"I know. I talked to her last night. I came to talk to you, but maybe I should wait until you are finished sobering up."

She put her hands on her hips. "I am perfectly sober, thank you very much, and my headache is almost completely gone. What's up?"

"I've taken a job, and I don't think you are going to be happy about it."

"Since when do you consult me about jobs? Why should I care—" She paused and then breathed in a sharp breath. "You are working

39

for the pig who bought my farm, aren't you? Brandon!" She completed the exclamation with a stomp of her foot. "How could you be such a traitor? I suppose he's paying you nicely to build his hipster lemonade stand."

"What? Lemonade stand? You *are* still drunk. I don't see the guy sitting on the porch squeezing lemons for all the customers he'll have out in the middle of nowhere. He is fixing up the house and plans to do much of the work himself, but somethings are beyond his skill."

"Sounds familiar." Tara wanted to throw something. She'd had a nice morning, and then the reality of her situation came crushing back in the form of her backstabbing cousin.

"I'm not a traitor, Tara. I'm a man in need of a paying job. I can't afford to turn this one down because of sentimentality. Winter is coming, and all the work will be dried up until spring. I'd like to pay my bills the next few months and not feel guilty about it."

She let out a frustrated sigh. "Damn it. You are as pragmatic as Charlotte. Why won't anyone just let me be angry about this?"

"Because we care about you and understand the family dynamic enough to know you're heading straight down the road to Franville, and you know what a witch your mother is when she doesn't get her way. We've all tried hard not to be like our parents. Don't slip now."

Tara's shoulder's slumped. Not wanting to have the same argument she'd had with

40

her sisters, she changed the subject. "We were spawned from a generation of assholes, weren't we?"

Brandon smiled and nodded. "Yes, but we're grown now, Tara, and are responsible for ourselves."

"Yeah, yeah. Save your sermons, father. Hey, can you watch the counter for a minute? I want to go run a brush through my hair."

"You really should. I was just about to say it looked pretty ratty."

She stuck her tongue out at him and walked to the back room, where she pulled out her purse, brushed her hair, and applied what little makeup she kept in her bag. Thankfully, the lighting in her aunt's shop was designed to make things look good, even a woman pushing thirty with clear signs of a hangover beneath her eyes. After she chewed on a couple sticks of gum long enough to be sure the last signs of the coffee she had drunk but barely tasted was sufficiently masked, she returned to the front, where Brandon was engaged in a friendly conversation with a man carrying a large to-go bag. They both turned to her, but only one smiled. Brandon rarely did so unless under extreme duress.

"Well, I'm going to take off. See you, Tara."

After shooting Tara an amused look and nodding at Justin, her cousin quickly vacated the shop. She was glad to have to skip the need to shoo him away. He would accuse her of being an asshole, again. Putting all thoughts of her traitorous cousin aside, she turned to Justin and smiled.

"So how was your tour of the town?"

"Interesting. I saw some familiar artwork in the gallery across the street. Your paintings are even lovelier than your jewelry."

She barely managed not to sigh. She was vain enough to be swayed by compliments on her art and honest enough to admit it, at least to herself. Everything about this man seemed genuine, though, so she allowed herself to be flattered without guilt. "Thank you. I love to paint, especially when the area provides such inspiration."

He smiled and placed the bag on the counter. "I know you said you liked Proud Larry's, but to be honest, I didn't like the looks of the place. I asked around, and a few people said Speedy's has the best specialty sandwiches in town. You are well known on Main Street, it appears. It wasn't hard to find out your favorites."

Tara didn't know which thought flying through her head to concentrate on first. She settled on the slight indignation she felt toward his dismissal of Proud Larry's. The owners had come to town a few years ago and turned the restaurant into a spot that wasn't weighed down by trying to appeal to tourists. It was an eclectic place, with nudes on the walls and a rather interesting fresco of dogs playing hopscotch. At first glance, it could be easily dismissed as a hippy hole in the wall. She decided to let that

42

pass, figuring he'd get in the swing of things once he settled into the place.

The second thought that came forward was slightly more alarming. "Who did you ask?" *Don't be Fran. Don't be Fran. Don't be Fran.*

"She was standing behind me when I asked the clerk if she knew you. I didn't get her name, but she had long black hair and green eyes a lighter shade than yours."

Tara was only a little relieved. "That's my sister Charlotte. She is going to rag me all night about the hot guy buying sandwiches."

A corner of his mouth tilted, and she refused to be embarrassed by the slip up. He *was* hot, and no way did he not know that.

"The two of you don't look much alike."

Tara walked to the door, closing but not locking it. Customers could still come in, but she would be alerted by the bell. She then gestured for Justin to follow her to a small break room.

"She's my stepsister. Her father married my mother when we were all in college, but we grew up as friends. I live with her and my sister Shelby just up the hill."

"In the house with the amazing views." He started unpacking the bag, and she was relieved to see her second favorite sandwich appear. Her actual favorite was filled with onions and garlic. She owed Char for that one.

"You seem to have some investigative skills. I assumed you moved here to work at the university, but now I wonder if you are a cop or a lawyer."

43

"Well, you are almost right. I *was* a lawyer. I quit my job before I moved here."

"Is that a hint that I should pay for my half of lunch?"

He laughed, and she swallowed hard, admiring the little lines in the corners of his eyes. Happy lines. He was getting more and more appealing.

"I'm not destitute, yet, and I am accustomed to more expensive lunches."

"Lobster and Cristal?"

"No, sandwiches that cost twice as much. I moved here from Manhattan."

That was surprising. She would not have figured he was from such a large city. He seemed more homegrown. "That's a big change."

"That was the idea—to eliminate some of the noise and have a simpler life."

"And being a lawyer didn't give you that life?"

"No. I like law. I respect it. It appeals to the part of my nature that appreciates order and knowing where things fit, but I was never going to give impassioned speeches about it the way you do with your art."

"And you didn't figure that out while in law school? I only needed one semester to figure out I wasn't going to be an accountant."

His smile was rueful and a bit guilty. "I was in law school for the wrong reasons. I applied and then worked my ass off to graduate with honors just so I could join a rival firm and piss off my old man."

"That's quite a commitment to pissing someone off. Did it work?"

"It did. He didn't speak to me for two years and cut me out of his will."

He was dressed casually but expensively, so Tara figured the financial loss didn't hurt him much.

"Did you ever face him in court?"

"No, thankfully. He would have mopped the floor with me. What he lacked in substance, he made up for in style. He knew the law well and could deliver that knowledge in a way that could cast doubt on even the most damning evidence. He was a master manipulator and a controlling bastard. That's probably more information than should be shared on a first date."

Date. She had to tramp down the sudden rush of nerves that word caused. "Don't be uncomfortable. There must be something about me that screams 'Tell me all your troubles, even the ones no one needs to know about.' You wouldn't believe the things people tell me, and not even people I know well. Total strangers will just unload right after saying 'how do you do.'"

"Is that a hint that I need to shut up?"

She giggled. A giggle from a near thirty-year-old with a hangover could not sound alluring. "No, not at all. In fact, I'll reciprocate with *my* daddy issues. My father couldn't be called controlling, but bastard is accurate. My parents divorced when I was twelve. He's a history professor, and he took a position in

Charleston, where I'm sure one of the perks for him is having access to young college girls with their own daddy issues."

"Something he has in common with my father. My sister was born when I was eighteen, to a woman only five years older than me. I didn't even know about her until almost a year later. He was still married to my mom at the time. What about your mother? You said your stepfather is the mayor, so she must have remarried."

"She did, several years after she dropped me and my sister with my grandmother, who had just lost her husband, while she moved to Europe to reinvent herself. It took about six years, but she managed it. At least enough to snag one of the richest men in town when she returned. So there. We are now even on first date inappropriateness."

He laughed as he tossed his empty wrapper in the bag. Then, taking her hand in both of his, he gave her a slow, easy smile, making her insides flop.

"You are a kind woman, Tara, to tolerate such rambling from a man you barely know."

She wanted to speak, but her wit escaped her. She was too caught up in the gentle warmth of his eyes and his hands cupping hers. None of her previous boyfriends, all two of them, had affected her so easily. He brought her hand to his lips and then rose from his chair, his eyes now showing a trace of something wicked that took that warmth straight to boiling.

Justin's eyes roamed hers and then slid down to her mouth. He wanted to kiss her, and she held her breath, waiting to feel him reach for her. He didn't. Instead, he tugged at her hand until they were standing side by side and finished clearing the table.

"So I have daddy issues, no job, and there's the sister I keep telling you about. Still, I would like to see you again if you aren't scared off."

Tara smiled. This was what she needed. Something new, and gorgeous, to look forward to. "Not scared. I have my own daddy issues, my mother certainly wouldn't call art a job, and I have two sisters I haven't warned you enough about. Sounds like we're pretty even."

He took her hand again as he made his way to the door. "Well, I may not be employed, but I do have quite a job on my hands. The place I just bought needs a lot of work. Is it impolite to ask how you are with a hammer?"

Tara began to speak but stopped in her tracks. Something about his words sent a chill of realization through her. "What?"

"I'm only joking. I hired that guy Brandon to do some of the harder jobs, but I still plan to get my hands dirty, at least some."

"You hired Brandon?"

"Yes. That wasn't a mistake, was it? His references were excellent."

"You bought the farm?"

Of course he did. Unemployed lawyers didn't sweep into town for no bloody reason.

"I did buy a farm. It's out of town a way but has great potential."

This was him. The guy whose money was more important than her dreams. She pulled her clammy hand out of his.

"Are you okay?"

She stepped back. "Fine. Maybe that isn't my favorite sandwich after all."

Her stomach was certainly roiling, but not from lunch. She tamped down the urge to scream, instead allowed all the resentment she felt since the first time she lost the house serve as her shield against another disappointment.

"I don't—"

"I'm sure you have things to do, and so do I. I don't want my aunt thinking I'm a slacker."

Before he could say anything, she guided him out the door and then turned away, not looking back to see if there was any of the regret in his eyes that she was determined not to feel.

Chapter Six

The parking lot of the local farm co-op/building supply store was filled with dirty SUVs and old pickup trucks. Justin's European sports car looked as out of place there as it did on the farm. He would have to replace it with something more practical soon, but for now, he stuck out like the city boy that he was.

As soon as he walked in, Justin spotted Brandon by the counter and, as he moved toward him, could see that he was talking to a group of men, all of whom were eyeing him as he came closer. He nodded when he reached them and then waited a moment for Brandon to introduce him. He did not. He just eased off the counter and took two steps back and gestured to a cart next to him.

One of the men laughed and pushed his worn baseball cap back from his forehead. "If you're waiting on Brandon there to have some manners, you might as well stop. The boy has none. His poor grandmother complains about it all time. The dear girl is often in need of comforting."

Brandon scowled. "Stay away from my grandmother, Willie."

The older man blew out a breath and shook his head. "Time goes too fast. One day fathers are warning you away from the pretty girls, and the next, it's their grandsons who're keeping an eye on you." He held out his hand, and Justin took it with a slight smirk. "Will Hester. You must be the man who bought the old McNair place."

"If you mean the farm off Highway 64, that's me."

"That's the one. The McNair family owned it for more than a hundred years, so you'll likely hear it called that as long as it's yours. What are you planning on doing with the place?"

Justin slid his hands into the pockets of his jeans. "Well, today we'll be working on the attic floors and maybe sanding the beams."

"What about the farm?"

"I have no idea."

Will laughed. "That land has gone unused for a while now. It's going to need some work, whatever you do. You might consider getting some goats for the field."

Justin couldn't decide how to interpret the man's advice, so he decided to ignore it and ask what he really wanted to know. "What did the McNairs do?"

The man shrugged. "A little of everything, but really just enough to feed themselves and then the girls Mary was raising. They'd sell at

50

the farmers' market, but George always had jobs on the side. I wouldn't get my hopes up if you are planning on making any money off it."

Justin might not have his cousin's instincts, but he knew when he was getting sized up. It annoyed him, as everything had the last few days.

"Right now, I'm just concentrating on getting the house fixed up. Everything else will come in its own time."

Brandon thankfully had had enough of the conversation, too. "All right, Willie, we have work to do. You can save your gossiping for another day."

"See what I mean, no manners. You boys have a good day."

Justin nodded and then turned to follow Brandon, who had taken the cart toward the back of the store. He stopped in front of a large pallet of the wood flooring they had previously picked out and began stacking cases of it onto the cart.

If there was a classic image of a mountain man, Brandon fit it. He was taller than Justin by a few inches, and with his faded jeans, work boots, and flannel shirt, he could pass for Grizzly Adams any day of the week. The shaggy dark hair and beard made him all the more authentic.

"Willie's more full of shit than the fertilizer section, but he doesn't mean any real harm. He's just trying to get the scoop on your financials and marital status because, so far, it's all conjecture.

Well, your financials anyway. Everyone assumes you're not married after the way you went after Tara." He narrowed his eyes and stood up straight. "You're not, are you?"

"No, I'm not. I didn't 'go after her.' We had lunch. It doesn't seem to matter anyway since she blew me off." He had seen her a couple of times around town. Each time, she firmly ignored him. He had no idea what he had done, and the confusion irritated him.

Brandon rubbed the back of his neck and relaxed his stance. "Yeah, sorry about that. Tara's been going on for weeks about the asshole who stole everything she ever wanted. We're all pretty sick of hearing about it nonstop, and I thought it'd be funny to see her realize you're actually a decent guy. How pissed was she?"

Justin dropped the last case of wood onto the cart. "What are you talking about?"

"Did you tell her about buying the farm?"

They walked toward the paint section to pick up the off-white paint Marley had picked for her walls.

"I did, and right after, she pushed me out the door."

Brandon's expression tightened. "Tara made an offer on it, but yours blew hers out of the water. It was her grandparents' place. She was raised there after her folks ran off."

Justin's stomach dropped to his knees. "Shit."

"She didn't yell at you about it?"

"I get the feeling she's not the yelling type."

Brandon nodded and pressed his lips together. "Yeah, you're probably right. Tara's more of a let the resentment fester and eat away at you kind of girl rather than the type to explode and then come to her senses. That's more Charlotte's style."

They were quiet for a moment as they loaded more supplies. Justin was relieved to know why she had turned on him, but it did not lessen his disappointment. "So how do I fix it?"

"Fix it?"

"Yeah. How do I get past the resentment? You seem to know her pretty well. You must have some idea of how to go about it."

"She's my cousin. Fixing things with women isn't exactly something I'm good at."

Justin could believe that. "Come on. You must be able to give me some clue."

Brandon shook his head. "Tara can hold a grudge better than anyone I know. Though she is usually rather sensible, she was determined to have that farm even though she couldn't afford it and the repairs would be more than she could handle. For her to have wanted it that badly, she's not going to get over her indignation for a long while."

"You're not very encouraging."

"You want smoke blown up your ass, go talk to Willie. Look, man. Tara hasn't brought enough men around for me to know how she behaves around them. I got no advice except a warning that it could take some time. If you are going to be around and not lose interest like the last owners, you've got that. Tara loves this town. If you're part of it, she might learn to tolerate you, too."

Tolerate. That wasn't exactly what he had been hoping for.

"How did her family lose the place to begin with?"

Brandon stopped loading the cart and looked Justin over as if he were deciding whether or not he was worthy of the family secrets. The sizing up business was getting old.

"Their grandfather died before Tara and Shelby went to live there, so it was just their gran and them after Fran and Michael took off."

"Fran and Michael are their parents?"

Brandon nodded. "After they divorced, Michael took another job and moved to Charleston. Fran stayed in town a while longer, causing trouble. Michael's parents were still living then, and Fran was an embarrassment to them. They paid her to leave town. She did and left Tara and Shelby with Mary."

"How old were they?"

"Twelve and fourteen, I think. Fran stayed away for six blessed years. When she came back, presumably after the money ran out and Michael no longer had to pay her child support, the girls were away at college, and Mary was sick with some sort of lung disease."

"And Fran pounced."

"Yep. She took up with Tom Jackson, who

had just lost his wife to cancer, and managed to get a legally binding will signed and filed before anyone got wind of it."

"So the mayor is a crook, too?"

"I wouldn't say that, exactly, but I've never known anyone who's led by his dick more than him, and Fran's got a good hold on him."

"Did they not know their grandmother was sick?"

"Whenever they would call, Mary would downplay everything, and Fran didn't tell them the truth either."

"Why? What would she have to gain by lying to them?"

"I can't say for sure, but I think she was jealous. If you had seen the farmhouse before Fran fleeced it, you could easily see how important the girls were to Mary. She doted on them. Fran had always preferred to be the center of everyone's attention and could get ugly if she wasn't. Charlotte finally got wind of what was happening and called them home. They were at least able to say goodbye."

"And Fran sold the farm?"

"And everything in it—vintage pieces, antiques as old as the house, all the livestock and farm equipment. Tara and Shelby didn't even have mementoes left. Shelby begged Fran not to go through with the sale, and Tara just seethed, knowing that if Fran had dollar signs in her eyes, there was no reasoning with her."

"And then a couple from Florida bought it,

visited a couple of times, and then ignored it completely."

"Pretty much."

They had made their way through the checkout and out to Brandon's truck, where they unloaded everything onto the bed.

"This is a small town. If even the old men at the co-op gossip, then surely everyone knows about this. How did Jackson get elected?"

"This area is pretty much split into threes. There're the old timers and the families who have been here for generations, the new blood that the university brings in, and the ones who live here for three quarters of the year but claim residency and have registered to vote. Those last two tend to see party affiliation more than character. You heading straight to your place?"

"Yeah, I'll be right behind you."

Justin folded himself into the car, digesting what Brandon had just told him. He shouldn't feel so much regret and anger for someone he barely knew, but he did. Tara had experienced a miserable childhood, much as he had, and then found a place to belong, only to have it ripped from her—twice. If not for Marley, he'd sell the place to Tara, whatever the loss was. But he truly believed this would be a place of healing for his sister, especially after seeing her reaction to the attic. He would not give that up, not for an attraction that was obviously going nowhere.

Chapter Seven

Tara shifted the box of supplies to her hip so she could knock on the door of her friend's classroom. Liz Shaw looked up from her desk and smiled, quickly coming to the door.

"Hi. Do you need a hand?"

"No, just tell me where to put it."

Liz led her to a long table beside her desk that held two slow cookers filled with melted soap starter. Tara placed the box on the table and started pulling out items. Liz taught sixth grade at Sylvan Hills Junior High and had Tara come in twice a semester for arts and crafts projects. While the school did have art classes, both budget restrictions and the lack of motivation of the aging art teacher limited the variety of what the students learned. Liz believed that if kids were exposed to enough of the world, they would find something of it that they enjoyed, and that is especially true of art.

So armed with a small budget supplied by her aunt, Tara planned easy and fun lessons with an attempt to tie in to whatever Liz was teaching in other subjects. Because their history lessons were now in an era where the trend in hygiene was no hygiene, Tara thought soap making was appropriate.

"I hope you know what you are getting into, Liz. Your classroom is going to stink of perfume for at least a week."

Liz's short blond curls shook when she laughed. "I am so glad you chose soap. I don't know what it is about this age group, but it seems they all forget the importance of not stinking, bless them."

"I'm glad I could help you out. If nothing else, the essential oils will mask the funk for a while."

"I haven't seen you around town much lately. Anything interesting going on?"

"Just working on producing enough pieces to sell during the busy season. I've been helping Lady in the shop quite a bit as well."

"So no new man warding off the chilly October nights?"

Tara stopped arranging bottles and looked at her friend through slanted eyes. "Okay, what have you heard?"

"Nothing! I'm serious. I had not heard anything, but your reaction certainly has me curious."

"There's nothing to be curious about, unfortunately. I did have a date recently, but it didn't work out."

The fact that it made her sad annoyed the

hell out of her. As she had predicted, her sisters had teased her mercilessly when she got home that night. Shelby refrained from calling her a fool for passing on a great guy for the sake of old hurts, but Tara could see the accusation in her eyes. Charlotte had, surprisingly, been more understanding.

"It's not always easy to let go. Sometimes, whatever is blocking the road is just bigger than what's on the other side."

She was glad to have at least one person on her side. Brandon had texted an apology of sorts for letting her walk into the situation unaware, accompanied by another warning about her potential asshole-ness. It was only a matter of time before Lady joined the debate.

"That's too bad. It'd be nice to see you with somebody."

"What is it with you married people? You're always wanting to see your friends get tied down, too."

She smiled wryly. "Misery loves company? I don't know but you're right. I just don't like the idea of anybody being lonely."

"Why would you think I am lonely?"

Before Liz could answer, the bell rang, and the throng of students began lining inside from the playground. Tara moved behind the table and continued to set up her supplies as she watched the students come through the door. She remembered sixth grade too well. It was the year her parents divorced, and both split town soon after. She became a mouthy, moody annoyance, and if not for her grandmother's attention, she would have likely traveled a different path.

A group of girls came in together, and Tara's memories shifted to something far more pleasant—her sisters. Though these girls were all the same age, they had the same sweet mischievousness about them that she remembered sharing with her sisters. Just behind them was a small-framed girl with a look of longing that nearly broke Tara's heart.

The girl was dressed in dark colors, contrasting against her pale skin and light blond hair. Her eyes were so dark they could have been black, giving her an otherworldliness that would drive the boys crazy in a few years. Now it just came across as awkward. Though the contrasting hair and eye color were reversed, Charlotte had that same type of look about her.

Her arms were crossed in front of her as she walked, and the stance went as well with her facial expression as her clothes did with her hair. Tara's mouth formed a thin line as she went back to her task. Once everyone was seated, Liz introduced her, and she began giving oral instructions to go with the written ones Liz handed out.

"Two things you need to remember are that the soap base is hot, so please be careful. And also remember that with the essential oils you are using to scent your soaps, a little goes a long way. I've included some scent combinations on your instructions that you might want to use. The oils not only smell good but can also positively contribute to your moods. For instance, lavender is relaxing, and mint is rejuvenating.

"If you want to have the soaps for bathing, you should probably use the bigger molds, but if you prefer to use them to scent your drawers or closets, the smaller ones work well. We also have decorations you can add once your soap has hardened a bit. Dried flowers and citrus peels. There's also small rubber ducks if you have younger siblings you'd like to give the soap to. Any questions?"

The kids all looked a little dazed, and she wondered if she had gone too fast. She wasn't a natural-born teacher, though she did enjoy helping Liz with these projects. She had talked too much, she realized. Hands on was always best with kids and art.

"Why don't you come up a few at a time to smell the different oils and get an idea of what you might like to use."

Liz smiled in approval. "Good idea, Miss Tara. Let's have the first row, please. And do be careful not to spill."

Five at a time, the students came up, some enthusiastic, others not so much. She tried to teach the kids about scent and color combinations but could not tell if they were listening. How did Liz do this day in and day out?

"This age group rarely shows excitement about anything. It wouldn't be cool," Liz whispered to her as the last group lined up at the table. Tara saw the blond girl smelling the lavender with a grimace. Everyone around her was talking and giggling, but she held herself off to the side. As if anyone with her uniqueness could ever be invisible. Tara decided to dive in and talk to her.

"Do you have a question about something?"

"Um, yeah. You said lavender was relaxing. Is there anything that can do that but smells... more for a guy?"

"What's your name?"

"Marley."

"Marley, try this one. It's bergamot. Not very exciting on its own, but it smells nice with sandalwood. Both can help with anxiety."

The girl nodded and gave a small smile before moving down to look over the decorations. Tara thought she saw a playful gleam in her eyes as she looked at the rubber ducks, but it disappeared quickly as she turned to go back to her seat.

Tara's eyes roamed over the class, taking in some familiar faces, even if all she recognized were particular traits that were strong in the families she knew. The jet-black hair and green eyes that were common to all of Charlotte's mother's family were featured in the boy in the front row. There were kids whose parents she had known in high school, like Molly Taylor. Her parents were ahead of her, but she knew them through Shelby.

Tara realized she knew of most of these kids, but not Marley, though she did somehow look familiar. Once the soaps were mixed and poured, she had the students place their projects on the old radiator under the window and clean up any mess they had made. She used the opportunity to quietly ask Liz about the girl.

"I don't recognize Marley from anywhere in town."

"You wouldn't. She just moved here from New York. Her mother died earlier in the year, poor thing, and her brother is now her legal guardian."

Tara's skin prickled. Justin had not said he was raising his sister. Perhaps he implied it, but she was too busy lusting after him to notice.

"She seems sweet."

"Mmm-hmm. And rather shy. I've tried to encourage her and Molly to talk, but so far, neither of them have bitten."

Molly's stepfather had died earlier in the year as well. His cancer had come on fast and hard, and he was gone within months. Molly's dad still lived in town, but her stepdad had been in her life since she was five.

Tara could not help but wonder about the girl. Perhaps it was just knowing she was Justin's sister that had her curious, but she didn't think so.

Soon, the bell was ringing to signal the end of the day. The soaps would need to set for several days, but then they could unmold them and take them home. She told Liz as much as she stacked up the things on her desk.

"I'm sorry to leave you to pack up by yourself, but I have carline duty. You probably want to wait until all that is over before you carry your things out to the parking lot. Give it twenty minutes or so, and then all that will be out there are teachers and parents waiting for their kids to get out of band."

Tara hugged her friend once more before Liz hurried from the room with a walkie-talkie in her hand. After she packed everything back into the box, she walked over to where the kids had placed their molds. Most of them were silicone and would release easily, but Tara decided to ask Liz if she could come back to help unmold and package the soaps in case there were any difficulties.

She leaned in to smell a few. Liz was right. In spite of her efforts to monitor the oils, some of the students had indeed been generous while pouring. Thankfully for Liz, the windows could open. She looked at one set of molds in various star patterns, the ones she had seen Marley use. Had she made these for her brother? She breathed in and could clearly pick up the scents Marley had used. Just how much did the man need to relax? He had not seemed overly anxious during their lunch, but she supposed he could just be good at hiding it.

The thought that he was keeping things to himself was far more comforting to her than the idea that he had been so comfortable with her that he spoke of his family issues and made her feel that nothing was more important in those moments than her.

She abruptly turned from the soaps to gather her box and head out the door, fiercely determined not to think about the man another minute, except to continue to hate him for stealing her future. That determination lasted all of two minutes. As she walked through the doors to the parking lot, she saw him leaning against an expensive foreign car, looking lean and gorgeous as the wind caught the waves of his hair. Marley's hair was a few shades lighter and her eyes a different color, but the resemblance between them was easy to see. He caught sight of her and smiled before lifting himself off the car and heading her way.

"Let me help you with that."

"I don't need—" Her protest died as he took the box from her arms and looked down on her with an eager expression, like a puppy seeking approval. She resisted the urge to pet him and, instead, pulled her keys from her pocket.

"Thank you."

"Do you work here, too?"

"No, I volunteer in my friend's classroom a few times a year." She didn't offer anything further as she opened the trunk of her much older domestic clunker.

"Listen, Brandon told me about the farm, that it had been in your family and you had wanted to buy it." He sighed and ran a hand through his hair. He looked nervous enough now. Perhaps she should pull out the bergamot. "I knew there was another offer on the table. I'm sorry you were hurt by the deal."

Tara closed the trunk. Hard. "Well, it doesn't matter anymore, does it?"

"It does matter because you despise me for it. Do I have to be the bad guy? Can't I just be the man you got to know in the backroom of your aunt's store. The one who thinks you are beautiful and fascinating and really wants to spend more time with you."

He had taken her hand at some point, and his thumb, gently rubbing against her palm, sent jolts straight to her stomach. She pulled back in an effort to concentrate on her anger rather than the plea she saw in his eyes.

She nodded to his car and leveled as much of a glare as she could manage. "You're also a man who throws money around to get what he wants, regardless of who might be hurt by it. I've had enough of that in my life." She turned to open her door and got in, looking back up to him as she started the car. "Besides, you have enough on your plate. You have a farm to renovate."

He also had a sister who looked as lost as a lamb without its mother. Marley's eyes showed the same bewilderment when she asked about the scents as Justin's had when he bought the bracelet. Even through her anger, Tara had a helpless curiosity as to why.

Chapter Eight

After dinner, Marley disappeared to her room, and Justin sat at the kitchen table, nursing a cooling cup of coffee and replaying his interactions with Tara over and over in his head, preferring to concentrate on their lively conversation the day they met rather than their encounter earlier that day. He told himself for the hundredth time that he was being ridiculous. He barely knew her. Still, disappointment curled through him.

It wasn't only physical, though there was a good deal of lust present in his musings. She was beautiful, sexy, the kind of woman who walked into the room and you could immediately hear the Commodores playing in your head. Her appeal was so much more than that, though. His cousin Josh had teased him about mountain women, that they'd be all resilience and little grace. From what he saw, Tara had plenty of each along with a humor and warmth that made him want to laze in her presence, like a cat stretched out by a warm fire.

Justin rolled his eyes and rose to put his mug in the sink. Anyone reading his thoughts would think he wasn't a grown man but some silly teenage boy pining for his first love. He had enough to think about without obsessing over a woman who was determined to hate him. Like the sister who was determined to hate him, or at least dislike him enough to flee from his presence as much as possible. It annoyed him almost as much as it frightened him.

Defiantly, he yanked a permission slip off the fridge and sat down to fill it out. Marley's class was going to Green Energy Park the next week, and they needed chaperones. Though she was likely to shoot him the stink eye the entire time, he would take her and as many classmates as he could fit in his car. This wall between them had to come down somehow, and more time together could only help expedite it.

Just after he signed the bottom of the form, a ping sounded from his phone, alerting him to a text. He rose again to retrieve his phone from the counter and smiled when he saw it was from Ann.

"I assume that if you've been kidnapped by banjo-wielding mountain folk to be used to provide additional DNA, I would have heard about it on the news. Since I haven't, you must be alive and well???"

Justin shook his head and hit call. Such willful ignorance deserved a conversation.

"Hello."

"You of all people should know better than to perpetuate such stereotypes."

Ann laughed, and Justin felt his spirits somewhat lift.

"I'm sorry. Are the inbred now on the list of things we can't tease about? Society will soon crumble if we can't make fun of the world we live in."

"And you believe I live among the inbred."

She laughed again. "Josh was over for dinner tonight, and we talked so much about you behind your back that I thought you deserved a little of it to your face, er, over the phone."

"I appreciate you keeping me in the loop, Annie. How are you feeling?"

She groaned. "This baby has no idea that morning sickness is supposed to be confined to mornings. I can't seem to go two hours without feeling the need to hurl. My doctor says I shouldn't let my stomach get empty. Garret calls about fifty times a day to tell me to get an apple."

"Why does that annoy you?"

She sighed and was quiet for a moment as if trying to find the right words. "Okay, you are probably the only person in the world I can say this to without sounding like a complete bitch. He's driving me crazy, Justin. He is treating me like the most fragile thing in the world, and you know how I hate that. When did my Gucci-wearing husband turn into an alpha male hell bent on protecting what is his?"

"Maybe this is just the first time you've let him protect you. You are so used to fighting for yourself that you don't always know when to accept help."

"You know that for me, help often comes with tags like 'pity' or 'admiration.' It's just easier not to deal with it."

"And has Garret ever once treated you like that?"

"Of course not. I wouldn't have married him if he did. I'm just saying I'm not in the habit of needing a protector. I don't think I need one now, but he is determined not to see me upset, and nothing upsets me like my mother. He could tolerate her before, but they argue all the time now. Justin, I think she's sneakily trying to move in here. She keeps leaving random things behind when she visits—*everyday*. Scarves, her special anti-aging shake powders. I even found a toothbrush that didn't belong in the guest bath."

Justin could not help but laugh. He could see his aunt doing exactly that. She had never accepted Ann's independence, preferring to think of her as a delicate thing that needed constant supervision. It sounded as if she and Garret were fighting for the role of supervisor.

"I don't envy you, Annie, though I do have my hands full with Miss Silence."

"She's still not talking much, huh?"

"No, but I did see her laugh today. It wasn't with me, but at least it did happen." They had been painting the attic when a drop of paint landed in Marley's hair. Brandon told her not to worry about it, that it wouldn't show up in her white hair anyway. Marley laughed then. At Brandon.

"And she's taken a real interest in the house. I can't get out of her if she's made friends, but her teacher says she's always polite, if not talkative, and that it will happen eventually."

"What does her new counselor say?"

"That Marley is progressing at her own pace."

"Hmm. Are you getting impatient?"

"No! No, Marley can take all the times she needs as long as she is getting better."

"What about you? Are you making friends?"

"Yeah, sort of. The guy helping me with the house is…interesting. And, uh, there's this—" He sighed. "—girl."

He heard Ann's quick intake of breath and immediately regretted saying anything.

"I apologize for not supporting your move. You've barely settled in, and you've met a girl! Tell me all about her."

"Don't get too excited, Annie. Right now, it's all one sided."

"What? How could that be? You're the nice guy. The one every girl wants to marry. You're Henry Tilney bought to life for heaven's sake."

He had no idea who that was, but he knew that if his cousin wanted to insult him, she wouldn't be so vague.

"Doesn't do me much good when in her eyes I'm the villain. Hell, Annie, she's got cause."

"You can't have messed things up already. You're not as smooth as Josh, but you're no heel either."

No, he wasn't. Josh was the type of man women flocked to, no matter what he might have done. Tara wasn't the flocking type, though, so attempting to imitate his suave cousin wouldn't help.

"Things were messed up before I even moved here. This farm I bought had been in her family for more than a hundred years. She was attempting to buy it back when I 'threw all my money around' and bought it out from under her."

"Oh, how romantic!"

He couldn't have heard her right. "*What*?"

"When you get married, the farm will be hers again, only better because now it has you and Marley."

"Annie, you're really starting to freak me out. Have you been taking your prenatal vitamins? You sound as if every mineral has been sucked from your brain, leaving you capable of only nonsense."

"It's not nonsense. It's like a plot from a romance novel. The hero buys this old house that's full of secrets, leading him to find the love of his life."

"I think I remember that one from high school. There was a crazy wife in the attic who would escape and walk around the moors and knock on people's windows in the middle of the night."

A frustrated sigh came from the other end of the line. "Now you're mixing your Brontës. You might have a better shot with this girl if you picked up the right kinds of books once in a while."

"That's your advice? Read romance novels?"

"No, but what I'm going to say *is* going to sound lame. Be yourself and give her time. And grand romantic gestures never hurt either."

"I'd just end up making a fool of myself."

"Possibly, but that can be endearing, too."

"What grand romantic gestures does Garret make?"

"He just brought me cheese and crackers, so I won't get sick in the night, and his laptop so we can watch Netflix until I fall asleep."

Her voice sounded entirely too dreamy. "Thought you didn't like that stuff."

"I blame my mood on the hormones. Except for the stuff with my mother. That's all on her."

Justin laughed again. "Get to your binging. Tell Garret I said hi."

"Goodnight, Justin."

He put down his phone and then began washing the dishes, thinking he might binge a little himself before bed, or perhaps download one of the books Ann suggested. At this point, he needed all the help he could get.

Chapter Nine

"Do you know if any kids from your class are going to be here tonight?"

Justin watched Marley's shoulders shrug under the fox-eared hoodie she wore over a matching skirt that no twelve-year-old had any business wearing. His insistence that she wear dark leggings underneath it had not gone over well, but she acquiesced more easily than he thought she would. He supposed that could mean she was becoming more comfortable with him telling her what to do or that she had not been overly excited about the lack of length either.

"I heard some people talking about it."

He waited for a moment to see if she would elaborate. She did not. "Well, *I* heard people talking about it, too. Looks like we missed most of the trick or treating, so you should be able to find plenty of activities meant for kids your age."

Main Street was closed to traffic, so they walked in the street, looking around to see that most of the shops had put up Halloween displays and were serving treats for the kids as well. They walked the length of the street to the courthouse, where inflatables had been set up around hay bales displayed in a semicircle.

As they turned around and headed back up the street, still in silence, Justin's eyes wandered to the elaborate display in front of It's by Nature and to the trio of witches who seemed to be in charge of it all. The three of them stood beneath a large painted sign that said "Toil and Trouble" with a bubbling cauldron on the end that matched the one the middle witch was currently stirring. She certainly did not resemble the character he had seen in any rendition of *Macbeth*. Tara's normally wild waves were tamed into a slick sheath with an electric blue streak on each side of her face. She was dressed in all black, and the long gown hugged her in all the right places. If that dress had a slit along her leg, he just might have to hide in the car the rest of the night.

Tara caught his eye as it trailed over her, and though he expected a glare, her face showed a friendly smile instead. He made one step toward her as her smiled widened just a little.

"Marley! Come over and try our punch. We just made a fresh batch and forgot to put the toads in this one."

Marley rolled her eyes but walked over, and Justin followed closely behind. Tara handed Marley a cup and barely looked at him before handing him one, too.

"Are you having a good time?"

"We just got here. This is the first booth we've stopped at."

"Well, that's too bad. All the others are bound to pale in comparison." Another witch had stepped forward and offered the full-wattage smile that Tara was determined to keep hidden. "I'm Shelby, Tara's sister."

Tara nodded their way as she filled cups for another family. "Shelby, this is Marley and Justin."

He noticed a slight waver, but the smile never disappeared nor seemed forced. Justin was relieved that at least one sister didn't hate him.

"Come down here, Marley, and let me show you the games. If you play each one, you get a prize."

The sweet-faced brunette led his sister away, and Marley did not look back. He turned to Tara and smiled in spite of the chill coming off her.

"This is quite a display. You must have worked hard on it."

"It's mostly Shelby's doing. She's going to be the ultimate Pinterest mom one day." She finally looked at him, taking in his costume. "I never would have figured you for a cowboy."

"I thought it would be fun to dress up with Marley, but she was pretty unimpressed by it."

"That's because you're her brother. Believe me, every other woman out tonight is more that impressed."

Justin turned to witch number three, whom

he recognized from the sandwich shop. "You must be Charlotte."

"Aw, you've been hearing about me, huh?"

"I'd worry about that if I were you. He's working with Brandon."

Charlotte looked at him with apprehension shining in her eyes. He just grinned and mimicked Tara's teasing tone. "We've had many interesting conversations."

Charlotte's shoulders relaxed. "Now I know you're just messing with me. Brandon's never interesting, just honest."

Justin chuckled as she turned away to serve punch to a group of moony-eyed boys, giving him the opportunity to move closer to Tara.

"How do you know my sister?"

"Hers is the class I volunteer in."

"She didn't mention it, but that's not surprising, considering she never mentions *anything* that goes on in school."

"She's twelve. She's supposed to sulk and be embarrassed to be seen in public with cowboys."

He looked down to the end of the tables where Marley was standing silently in a small crowd of girls.

"I can handle the embarrassment. It's the silence that scares me."

* * *

Tara watched as Justin took a slow drink from his cup. She had noticed him the second he and Marley walked by. It would have been hard not to. Charlotte was right; he did cut an impressive figure in his western-cut shirt, jeans, and cowboy hat. Who knew a city lawyer could look so good playing dress up. It suited him. She allowed the idea to penetrate her resentment. Though she had never seen him in his other role, she could not deny that the simple country boy quality seemed genuine. Too much about him seemed genuine.

Any hope she had that Justin would lose interest in the farm and eventually be willing to sell it disappeared the day she met Marley. Tara couldn't fault him for wanting to give his sister a home. She only wished he had chosen a different one. The bitterness everyone else was so tired of was slowly giving way to grief—a bone-deep sadness that that part of her life was over and could never be duplicated in the ways she had hoped. Seeing him adjust so well to the role she had wanted should have made her feel better, but it didn't. Still, she would try. She didn't want anyone else accusing her of being like her mother.

"Brandon hasn't said anything about what your renovation plans are."

He studied her for a moment, as if he were trying to avoid any landmines. "Right now, we are concentrating on getting Marley's room ready. It's taken more work than we expected."

"Oh? Which room did she choose?"

"The attic, actually."

Tara smiled through the ache in her gut. "It's a good room. I used to go up there with an old lamp and sketch."

"Would you draw the view from windows?"

She nodded.

"I thought I recognized it. I've seen it in some of your paintings in the gallery."

"A lot of my work is inspired by the farm. Was, anyway. Charlotte says it's time for me to find something new."

"You are always welcome there, Tara. To sketch or paint. For any reason."

She looked at him for a moment and then moved to the tables. The crowd was currently centered around Charlotte, so she kept her hands busy tidying the games. Justin followed but remained on the other side. He obviously wasn't going to give up the conversation.

"It's not the same now."

"Why not? It hasn't belonged to your family in several years. I'm sure you were out there plenty of times when someone else owned it. Why should it be different now?"

"No one was living there before. I could still pretend it was mine."

"Tara. I really am sorry you lost something so important to you."

She looked up then, but the remorse in his eyes didn't relieve the grief that was surely shining in hers. "Why did you choose it anyway? You must have looked at other properties."

"I did. All over the country, in fact. But I thought Marley would be happiest here, in this community, with the slower pace and art and recreational opportunities. I might have found that somewhere else, but it felt right *here*."

Tara pressed her lips together and returned to the games. She could feel the moment Justin looked away. She lifted her eyes slightly to see that Marley had returned, handing Justin several small items she had chosen from the prize bin.

"Will you hold these for me?"

Justin nodded and crammed everything into his pockets. Tara noticed Marley tense somewhat as she looked at her brother. "I'm going to go do the scavenger hunt."

Marley's tight shoulders stiffened further as Justin's eyes narrowed. Tara was surprised when he spoke. The tightness in his jaw should have prevented it.

"Alone?"

"No."

Justin's eyebrows rose, and Marley sighed and pointed to a group of girls behind her. "I'm going with some girls from my class. It's just around Main Street. It shouldn't take long."

He was quiet for a long moment. Finally, he shook his head and relaxed his shoulders. "Of course. Have fun. Just keep your phone on."

Marley nodded and walked away. Justin kept an eye on her until she was lost in the crowd. He then turned back to Tara. "I have to remind myself sometimes that situations like this are one of the reasons I moved us here. She's used to being more independent, but I was not comfortable allowing her to roam the city the way her mother did."

"She can have more room to move here."

"That's the idea."

From what Tara just witnessed, Justin was having a hard time with that idea. "How long has Marley been with you?"

"Almost nine months. Her mother died in January, but I didn't know about it for a couple of months. Marley was in foster care when I found her."

"Oh my god. Was it hard for you to get custody?"

"I only have guardianship, and no, it wasn't that hard. But you probably don't want to hear about the good that can come from throwing money around."

She decided to take that jab gracefully. "Why didn't you know her mother had died?"

More genuineness, this time in the form of guilt, crossed his features. "I didn't keep up with Marley and her mother like I should have. I'm afraid I let my youthful resentment keep me from getting to know my sister. I had no excuse once the youth was gone. I only heard Sharon had died because I ran into one of my father's former partners, who had heard from someone else."

His regret was palpable, and Tara could not help the impulse to provide comfort. God, she was a sucker for a man who loved his kid. She reached across the table and placed a hand on his arm.

"You have her now, when she needs you most. That counts for a lot, Justin. Believe me."

He took her hand from his arm and, holding it gently, briefly brought it to his lips. They'd reached the end of the table, and he kept her hand in his as they stood there.

"I thought about you last week. I went with Marley's class to Green Energy Park. It was interesting and not just because I saw Marley actually speaking to her classmates. Their wood-fueled kiln was quite a sight. Do you ever use it?"

"I do. I fire most of my pieces at my studio, but some look better with the effect that comes from the ash of the wood."

"Where's your studio?"

"Behind my house. It's small, but I manage. You said Marley was interacting with her class? That's good. When I was there, she was quiet. She was still new then, maybe she just needed to get comfortable."

"I hope that's all it takes. I worry when she won't talk to me, which is pretty much all the time."

"You're both new at this. Just give yourselves some space."

"That's what I keep hearing. It's harder than you might think."

"Why?"

"Justin! You made it, and in costume even."

Tara and Justin turned to see Jennifer Adams, Molly's mom, dressed as a popular cartoon princess, a few steps away. She owned the local dance and exercise studio and was as lithe and graceful as any professional dancer. Tara had always liked Jenn and felt bad for all she had been through, first with her divorce from Molly's dad when they were only in their early twenties and then with the death of her second husband. But just then, as she graced Justin with a beautiful, warm smile, a bolt of malice went straight through her. Or maybe it was just gas. She *had* indulged in a candy apple earlier.

"Hey, Tara. Great Display."

"Thanks. You look great."

"Thank you. Alice insisted I wear it to match her, though it certainly fits a three-year-old's tastes better than mine. She's been on Jesse's shoulders all night, and I haven't even gotten a picture." She turned to Justin. "Our girls ran off together. Jesse wasn't too far behind them, so they shouldn't get into too much trouble, not that they would."

"I'm glad. I'm not entirely comfortable with Marley going off on her own."

Jenn gave him a familiar, knowing smile that had Tara trying to pull her hand away, but Justin held firm. "I thought as much. That's why I thought I'd let you know. I think I'm going to go find them and drag my little one off Jesse's shoulders and make her take a picture with me. You guys enjoy your night."

Jenn not so subtly looked at their entwined hands and headed up the street, leaving Tara feeling ridiculous. Jenn was a sweet, friendly woman who lost her husband in January. She certainly wasn't on the prowl. That she would care one way or the other left Tara quite irritated with herself.

"You know Jenn from the school, I guess?"

He nodded. "We were in charge of a group on the field trip last week. Jesse is her ex-husband?"

"Yes. Theirs is pretty much the poster family for co-parenting. Marley is in good hands, and she knows where to find you. Relax. Enjoy the festival. It only comes once a year."

She felt his thumb glide over hers. "Will you walk with me?"

Tara was surprised to find that she wanted to. "I shouldn't leave Shelby and Charlotte. It's not the same effect with just two."

"Of course you can."

"Don't be silly."

Tara's head whipped around at the sound of her sisters' voices. They were about two feet away, wearing no signs of guilt for listening to their conversation. She turned back to a grinning Justin.

"Come on. You're being nice to me. I don't want it to end just yet." He tugged her out into the street and turned up toward the courthouse. They walked through the crowd leisurely, not stopping at any of the booths, only enjoying the crisp fall evening.

"I've always been nice to you." Tara lied. "Too nice, probably."

"The day we met, perhaps. That day at Marley's school, maybe not so much."

His voice was light, but Tara could hear the trace of apprehension he was trying to hide. "Brandon must have given you the whole story. Can you blame me?"

"No, I can't. In your position, I would feel the same way. You must miss your grandmother very much."

"I do. As Gran was dying, my mother got rid of everything in the house. Even the sentimental items that were of no value to anybody but Shelby or me were gone by the time we got home. But I had taken my old sketchbook to school with me, so with that and my memories, I was able to recreate some of our life there through my art."

"And so it lives on. There are pieces of you and your memories in houses all over the country, I would imagine."

Tara shrugged. "I don't know about that, but I do like knowing that Fran didn't take *everything*."

They came to the courthouse lawn and sat on one of the hay bales. Without the heat of the crowd, she should have been cold, but Justin sat so close that she barely felt the chill. A quarter moon hung high in the cloudless sky, and Tara briefly wondered if they'd see a witch on a broomstick flying by. Perhaps Shelby or Charlotte would be up to it. She was too content where she was. She felt Justin brush her shoulder.

"I don't like being the villain, Tara. That was always my father's role. It was never supposed to be mine. I understand that you can't just shut off your feelings. If you're not ready for more right now, maybe we can at least be friends?"

Tara sighed audibly. His understanding released much of the pressure she had been feeling since they met. Though he still held her hand and his demeanor said he would prefer much more, friendship was something she could manage.

"Yeah, I think we can be friends."

His smile right then almost had her changing her mind about the "just friends" thing, but a sparkling twelve-year-old appeared, saving her from the moment.

"Hey, kiddo. You got your face painted." Justin finally released her hand as Marley handed him more treasures from her hunt.

She pushed her hair back from her face. "Yeah. All my friends got butterflies."

Tara laughed. "So you decided to get a dragon?"

Marley shrugged. "It has glitter in it. It's almost the same."

"Well." Justin rose and Tara followed. "We better get going. You've got school tomorrow."

Marley groaned but fell in line as they started walking. "Are we still going to look for light fixtures? I really hated all the ones at the box store."

"For the attic?"

Marley turned to Tara and nodded. "Everything we saw looked so plain."

"Says the girl who painted the walls and ceiling white."

It was dark, but Tara could easily see the eye roll Marley gave her brother. "That's why the accessories should be bold and colorful."

It was Justin's turn to roll his eyes, and Tara laughed. "Did you see the glass blowing demonstration when you were at Green Energy Park?"

"Yes!" Marley's dark eyes managed to look bright against the sparkly red of her face paint. "I was scared it would pop like bubble gum in his face."

"I'm sure he's glad it didn't. Anyway, the artist, Noah, has a small gallery in his studio in Dillsboro. I know he's done globes and lamps before. You might find something you like there."

"Can we go?"

Justin nodded. "Why don't we wait until Saturday? We haven't spent any time in Dillsboro. We can make a day of it." Tara felt him nudge her shoulder again. "You can join us. I'm sure you know the best shops for authentic local art."

"The best shop for local art is my aunt's, but sure, I can meet you. I'll call Noah to make sure he'll be there."

"Great. Let's go early and then have lunch. One less meal eaten at home is a good thing."

Marley's enthusiastic nod made Tara laugh again. Justin deposited her back at her cauldron with a kiss on the cheek and a promise to see her Saturday. She wasn't sure what this new friendship would bring, but she did know that as she watched him walk away, no friend had ever left her feeling so much anticipation or with a desire for a kiss on the cheek to have landed an inch to the right.

Chapter Ten

"Marley?"

"I'm up here."

The familiar refrain sounded, and Justin made his way up the newly built stairs to the attic. Any time he couldn't find her, that's where she was, measuring and plotting her space. Eventually, he would learn to look there first.

The room still didn't have a door, so he saw her immediately upon entering, sitting at the large window he and Brandon installed the day before, with a pair of binoculars over her eyes.

"What are you doing?"

She turned to him briefly before returning her gaze to the outside. "Looking out the window."

"I can see that. Are you looking for anything in particular?"

"Elk. Brandon said there's a herd close by and that they used to come into the yard so much that the old owners had to build that fence."

"Is he the one who gave you the binoculars?"

She nodded and kept patrolling. "He said

they don't move beyond the woods too much anymore, but when he has gotten close-ups of them, it's been around this time of year."

"Well. I'm sorry to pull you away from your elk hunt, but we need to get going. Tara will be waiting for us."

She placed her binoculars on the windowsill and looked at him. They had enjoyed a few days of goodwill between them with the only argument being the usual one over her excessive use of her phone. Still, the steady look she was giving him made him nervous. She must have decided not to speak because she started to walk away. Justin reached out to stop her.

"What is it?"

She pursed her lips and shrugged. "I was just wondering what you were planning for Thanksgiving."

Justin blinked. "We're barely into November. Do we have to think about that already?"

"I guess not." She was going for nonchalance, but it didn't quite work.

Justin blew out a breath. "I've never really thought about it much. I always went to my aunt's house for Thanksgiving. My mother didn't do much cooking. What about you? What did you and your mom do?"

In an uncharacteristic move, Marley tucked her hair behind her ear and looked down. She never talked about Sharon, and whenever Justin brought her up, Marley would try to change the subject.

"We usually just had Chinese food with other actors from whatever show she was doing at the time."

"We can see if the Chinese place in town will be open, if you want." She didn't say anything. "Or we could...cook?"

She shrugged again. "We can cook. You know, if you want."

He smiled. The kid wanted a real Thanksgiving dinner but didn't want to ask for it. "We had sandwiches last night for dinner, Marley. I'm not sure I'm up to cooking a huge meal."

"We can go simple and YouTube some things. Surely we can follow instructions."

There was too much question in her voice, reflecting his own doubt at their ability to pull it off, but she so rarely asked him for anything. How could he not give it to her?

"All right. You find some recipes, and I'll try not to kill us."

She laughed then, a little, but he still felt as if he had won some great victory. It was short lived, however, because as soon as they got into the car, the earbuds came out, and Marley stared out the window as if he didn't exist.

* * *

Dillsboro's Main Street was much smaller than the one in Sylvan Hills, but no less interesting.

It was more casual, Justin supposed, with the goods offered in the shop windows leaning more toward homemade than artisan. He figured it was the difference between being in your grandmother's kitchen and her closet full of vintage Chanel.

Marley pulled out her earbuds and leaned forward, nodding toward their left. "Is that a train station?"

He slowed almost to a stop and looked to where she pointed. "It's a depot of some sort. I wonder if it's still in operation."

"You can ask Tara. She's sitting right in front of it."

Justin pulled into a parallel space near the tracks in front of the depot. He saw Tara sitting on the steps. She didn't have a phone or a book in her hands, just a to-go cup and a soft smile on her face as she looked around. Fallen leaves surrounded her feet, and her green sweater contrasted all the brown around her. Her hair was back to normal and pulled away from her face with the wild waves cascading down her shoulders. Like the scenery around her, she looked warm and inviting.

If only. He fought back the thought. Her acceptance of him as a friend was more than he had hoped for, and he would be grateful. For now, anyway.

Marley beat him out of the car, and spotting her, Tara rose.

"I've been looking for your fancy sports car. You traded down."

Justin and Marley crossed the tracks as Tara pointed to the new SUV he'd yet to get tags for.

"I guess that depends on your point of view. Now that I can get down all the hills around here without the fear of sliding, I think I've traded up."

He leaned down and kissed her cheek, taking just a moment to linger. "Good morning. You smell like fall."

"What?"

He pointed to her cup. "Pumpkin?"

"Oh, yes. I'm actually getting a little tired of them and am ready to move on to peppermint. Don't tell Shelby, though. She has us on a specific holiday schedule. No peppermint mochas until after Thanksgiving." She shifted her gaze. "Hi, Marley."

"Hi."

Justin tilted his head slightly as he looked at his sister. Halloween night she was all smiles and giggles, talking to Tara as if she had known her forever. Now she would barely look at her. Tara didn't seem bothered by it, though.

"Noah won't be in his studio until this afternoon, so we can look around for a while, if you'd like."

Justin nodded and then pointed behind them to the depot. "Does a train stop here?"

"It does. A company runs train tours of the area. I'm not sure of the schedule anymore because it is geared more toward tourists. They have stops here so passengers can get off the train and explore the town. The real attraction, though, is the station in Bryson City. Their Main Street is bigger than Sylvan Hills', and the station is right in the middle of it. They decorate it beautifully for the holidays, especially Christmas, and have special excursions that even the locals enjoy."

"Sounds like something else we need to check out."

Marley gave a noncommittal "hmm" and turned to head back over the tracks to the sidewalk. They followed her slowly, letting her decide the schedule of their lazy Saturday morning.

"She's probably too old to appreciate the trains, but the station *is* lovely. You should take her next month."

"I will, and you will have to come with us. I'm finding it very beneficial to have a friend who knows the area so well."

"I'm sure Brandon could show you around just as well."

Justin snorted. "He's shown me plenty inside the co-op."

Tara laughed. "That's his world, right there among the old men. Is he working today?"

"I told him not to worry about it today since we wouldn't be there to help, but he was pulling onto the road as we were pulling out."

They caught up to Marley as she entered a cottage-style store specializing in Christmas ornaments.

"This morning she was asking about Thanksgiving, and now she's jumped to Christmas."

Tara smiled. "You need to get her on Shelby's schedule."

Marley had walked toward the back of the store where a huge artificial Christmas tree stood surrounded by several smaller ones, all displaying various types of ornaments. Tara joined her while Justin hung back, trying to find something of interest other than the way Tara smelled, and moved, and the way her eyes shone when she smiled. He gave up and found a seat close by and watched appreciatively while she talked to his sister.

"I'm coming to your class next week to show you guys how to make clay ornaments."

"Oh yeah? Will it be like the Play-Doh ones I made in kindergarten?"

Justin would have thought Marley was being rude if not for the smile on her face. Just how many moods was she going to go through this morning?

Tara laughed. "I certainly hope not, but you'll have to compare it to your old ones when it's done."

As she had earlier, Marley tucked her hair behind her ear and stared at the tree. "I don't have any of them. I don't have any of my old things. When my mom died and I was put in foster care, our building super came in and cleared out the apartment. I don't know what he did with anything. All I had were my clothes."

Justin started at that. He had asked her once if Sharon's things had been put into storage.

Marley had just said no, put in her earbuds, and that was the end of it.

"I don't have any of my old things either. I don't know what my mother did with them, but she certainly didn't keep them. You'll just have to start collecting from this year on."

Marley nodded then whispered, "Not these, though. They aren't very exciting."

"No, they aren't. They were probably all made in China. We'll be able to find you plenty of unique pieces that were made here. But right now is the perfect time to check out the chocolate shop. They serve free samples before lunch."

Justin watched as Tara looped her arm through Marley's, nodded to the girl behind the counter, and then exited the shop. He was still reeling from what his sister had said. He should have pushed more when he asked about Sharon's things, but Marley had seemed determined not to say anything, just as she always did when it came to her mother. He followed the girls out of the store but stayed on the sidewalk as they entered the chocolate shop.

Allowing his anger at both the super and himself to take over, he pulled out his phone, quickly finding the number he was looking for. It was probably too much to hope that he could find any of Marley's things, but he had to try.

* * *

The sight that greeted them as they exited the chocolate shop made Tara blink in confusion. Justin paced back and forth on the sidewalk, oblivious to the people trying to make their way around him. He had his phone to his ear and a look on his face that could have stripped the paint from the walls—fierce and determined, not in a scary way but as if he had everything that was good and right backing him up. Gone was the casual country boy that seemed to come naturally to him, and in his place was what she assumed was the role he played while living in Manhattan.

She watched him for a moment, but when he uttered words that made the few people around them turn their heads in his direction, she quickly turned to Marley, whose attention, thankfully, was directly on *her* phone.

"Hey, I thought we'd grab lunch at the tea shop just down there." She pointed to the restaurant just a few doors down. "It's probably a little delicate for Justin's tastes, but I think you'll like it. Why don't you go get us a table before the crowd comes in?"

Marley looked at Justin, who was still pacing furiously, and lowered her eyebrows into a V, almost mirroring the look Justin gave her on Halloween. Tara was touched seeing Marley's concern. Did either of them realize how much they meant to the other?

"Go on. I'll find out what's going on."

Marley nodded and walked away just as

Justin ended his conversation. He noticed Tara and then looked around.

"Marley is just right there. She's gone to get us a table at the tea shop."

Justin nodded and let out a breath as he came to stand beside her. "That was Marley's old super. He didn't appreciate my questioning his authority to dump all of Marley's stuff without her knowledge or consent."

A chilly wind whipped through the buildings as they started walking, but Tara didn't feel it. Seeing Justin act as Marley's defender had her melting.

"Did he say what he did with everything?"

"It's all gone, donated, he said. He claimed there was nothing of value there, but if there was, you can bet he sold it. He said Sharon was two months behind on her rent and that he was justified in clearing out the apartment."

She took his hand and squeezed it as they reached the open doors of the tea shop. "You tried, Justin. Marley will appreciate that."

He didn't look so sure as they found his sister and sat down. Marley had put away her phone and was looking at him apprehensively.

Justin sighed. "I called your super. He said he donated everything. I'm sorry, kiddo."

Marley shrugged and then picked up her menu. "It's not your fault."

Tara could tell that Justin didn't agree. She wondered if he realized that the guilt rolling off him made Marley even tenser, though she was trying to hide behind her menu. Tara couldn't stand it, and her voice likely sounded a few pitches too high as she tried to break the tension.

"So what do you guys think of the place?"

Justin looked around and smiled. "I'm sure the two of you like it a lot."

He put his hand on hers for a moment, expressing his appreciation. She gave him a small smile in return.

"Is that Shelby?" Marley's voice sounded beside her, and Tara's smile grew.

"I wondered if you would notice that. I painted it a few years ago, and the owners bought it from the gallery."

A watercolor of her sister hung on the far wall of the restaurant, surrounded by mismatched plates and saucers. Tara had been quite proud of the piece, but it made Shelby uncomfortable to see it hanging in the house, so Tara sold it.

"I didn't know you did portraits."

Tara turned her gaze back to Justin. "I don't, usually, but I just wasn't feeling it one day and needed to do something different. Shelby was sitting on the couch reading, and I started drawing her. I worked on the portrait off and on for a few months in between other projects. It's the only one I've done since art school."

"You don't like doing them?"

She shrugged. "I guess people don't inspire me as much as nature does."

The waitress came and took their order— delicate sandwiches and tea for Marley and Tara and the heartiest item on the menu for Justin, micro greens topped with grilled chicken. He would be hungry long before they finished at the glass studio.

"If you're good and promise not to tell my sister, I'll share the fudge I just bought with you."

Justin grinned and leaned as close to her as would be appropriate with Marley at the table, but it was enough to send a flash of heat through her. "Peppermint?"

She nodded slowly.

"I promise I won't say a word. You can trust me, Tara."

The look in his eyes gave weight to his words, and Tara found herself desperately wanting them to be true.

Chapter Eleven

Tara was antsy. She always got this way right before she started a new project. The problem, however, was that there *was* no new project. She had sat down a half a dozen times at the potter's wheel over the past week, and every time, the clay ended up as a tired ball spinning away on the wheel. She had nothing—no inspiration, no focus, and no plan. This time of year was always a little difficult, with her obligations to the community often taking up time she would spend creating, but never before had the block been so powerful. She had always been able to burst through simply by working. Put your butt in the seat every day, and the muse will find you. Now, however, Tara was even having trouble getting to the seat, choosing instead to watch movies or read late into the night, causing her mornings to be foggy and unproductive.

This morning, she was at the school, fighting through the thickness in her head as she helped the students with their crafts.

"That's really good, Molly. Are you going to give that to your dad?"

Tara stood beside the dark-haired girl who proudly showed off the 3D motorcycle she had carved out of clay the day before. Liz had graciously agreed to a two-part project, allowing the students to create their ornaments one day and paint them another, after the clay had been baked and cooled.

"He usually lets us put up a tree in his shop and teases Alice and me about putting sparkly, girly decorations up for the bikers. My brother always brings some of his cars to hang on the tree, but this year, Dad will have one of his own."

Jesse owned a bike shop a couple of towns over at the end of the infamous Tail of the Dragon, a curvy, winding road that attracted bikers from around the world. Tara could only imagine what the place would look like if Jesse gave the kids free reign, which he probably did.

"Tara, can you help me?"

Marley was on the other side of her friend, and as Tara walked to her, she could see the frustration on her face.

"What's wrong?"

"I can't get the colors right. I've already gone over the trees so many times that I'm not going to be able to fix them. I at least need to get the house right."

Marley had made a round ornament with a raised image of the farmhouse and trees in the background. Tara had been impressed with her skill and was saddened now to see her frustration take away from her enjoyment.

"No damage is ever irreparable, Marley. The trees are still salvageable. What if you add snow to the branches?"

"Does it snow here at Christmas? I want it to be realistic."

Tara smiled. At one point she, too, was focused on showing only what was real. She learned that sometimes covering up reality was the only way to manage the ugliness of it. Sometimes that required a lot of layers.

"Perhaps the reality of this scene is that it snowed. It can be whatever you want it to be. This is a representation of the real thing. You'll still be able to recognize it with the artistic touches."

Marley nodded and reached for a paintbrush. Tara looked around the classroom to see if anyone else needed help. Since no one seemed to, she stayed with Marley.

"Did you get the light fixtures set up?"

"Mmm-hmm. The electrician finished yesterday. They really do look great against the white walls."

"What do you have left to do up there?"

"Justin and Brandon are building a seat and shelves under the new window, and then I'll just need a door and furniture."

"We don't have many places for furniture here in town. That might require a trip to Asheville."

"You'll come with us, won't you? I really don't want to be alone with Justin in a furniture store. We'll end up with something as ugly as the couch he ordered for the living room."

Tara smiled. "I doubt that. You have great taste, and Justin will let you have whatever you want."

Marley paused her painting and her voice became quiet. "Yeah, he will."

The girl's eyes looked nothing like her brother's, but just then, a brief flash of guilt crossed them that *was* identical to Justin's.

"Why do you say that like it's a bad thing?"

Marley shrugged, and all emotion that had shown so plainly a moment before disappeared. She lifted her brush again and focused harder than before, seeming to give all her attention to the model of the farm, until it was as close to perfect as anyone could expect. For the rest of the morning, Marley only spoke when necessary, and her eyes remained hooded, hiding anything that might leak through. It made Tara inexplicably sad.

The feeling stayed with her the rest of the morning as she finished with the kids, loaded her supplies into the car, and drove away from the school and toward Saint Mary's, where she was meeting the planning committee for the community's Thanksgiving dinner.

The only Catholic church in Sylvan Hills was small, but their hall was large enough to host the yearly event. Each Thanksgiving saw a different church acting as host, but all faiths and walks of life were represented in both the gathered crowd and those committed to the planning.

Tara was already thankful for at least one

fellow committee member. Melanie Simms, the owner of Main Street Bakery and Coffee, always brought coffee and pastries to the meetings, and Tara could smell them as she walked through the door.

"Hi, Tara! How's it going?"

Mel was in her early forties and already an empty nester. Her daughter, Ellie, was finishing up her RN studies in Raleigh. Mel had served on every volunteer committee and board that Tara had in the past few years, and in spite of their age difference, the two had become good friends.

"Great now that I see you are here. What did you bring?"

"Leftover donuts. Father Alex favors them, so we made extras this morning."

Tara pressed the spout on the large to-go box with the shop's logo on the side, filling her cup with the best coffee in town.

"I love coming to these meetings with you. The coffee is always fresh, and you bring real cream. There's not a church in town who doesn't buy the artificial stuff in bulk."

Mel laughed, sending her blond ponytail bouncing. "Well, I don't think we'll need to rely too heavily on the good stuff today. Seems like everyone in there is in a mood. The company might not be pleasant, but at least we'll stay awake."

Tara groaned. The town's volunteers were primarily made up of the unattached and childless like her and older people whose families had flown the nest, like her aunt, whom she could hear behind the folding doors of the great hall. If Lady was there, then so were her cronies and hangers on, all of whom were rather—interesting.

"I swear it's like some sort of reverse adolescence or high school for the elderly. They gossip and tease more than Ellie and her friends did when they were fourteen. I can't believe I have to keep reminding them that we are in a church." Mel's voice was laced with amusement.

"Well, hopefully Father Alex will join us soon and they will behave."

"I don't know. I don't think a priest will intimidate them one bit."

Carrying a donut and sipping her coffee, Tara followed Mel through the doors to the long table set up by a row of windows. The view wasn't spectacular, just of the parking lot and the small neighborhood behind the church. Tara saw two women standing outside, watching as three children, who must be preschool aged, rode their small bicycles around in a circle. Many of the neighborhoods in town weren't bike friendly, and most kids came down from the hills to ride in the areas that had asphalt and sidewalks. A little pang rose in her heart as she remembered the times she and Shelby had torn through that very parking lot on their way to Charlotte's. Of course, no mother was protectively watching over them. They were largely on their own.

She placed her snacks on the table and gave her aunt a quick hug before sitting down. "Hi, everyone."

A chorus of greetings followed, and Tara smiled at each one of them, still attempting to shrug off the ache that continued to pester her after the experience with Marley. The table was filled with familiar faces. Dale Adkins was a widower in his late sixties and owned one of the local berry farms. Tara's grandmother took Shelby and her blueberry picking every summer, and then the three of them would can and bake for weeks.

Alma Gregory sat next to Lady and was her complete opposite in nearly every way. While Lady was petite and genteel, Alma was tall and rugged and in every way a mountain woman. She, too, was widowed, and her only son was one of the doctors in town. Shelby had dated him briefly before adding his carcass to the pile of unworthy men she had been amassing since high school.

Will Hester sat across from Tara, and after draining the mug in his hand, he looked at her with raised eyebrows. Tara braced herself.

"So, Tara, I hear you've been spending time with that boy from New York. He going to take your attention away from our local boys?"

Tara started at that. Not the comment about Justin, she'd expect that, but the idea that there were any local boys left in the area who weren't related to her in some way or whom Shelby and

Charlotte had not already gone through. Pretty much everyone her age was a transplant. She shook her head.

"There's no danger of that, I'm afraid."

He leaned in slightly. "So you two aren't becoming friendly, taking advantage of some early mistletoe action?"

"Will Hester, do not embarrass my niece with your insinuations. You are in a church. Do not use the same talk you would at the co-op."

"Now, Lady, I'm just concerned about the girl. I assure you, dear, that we do not say such mild things at the co-op. If you are interested in what we do say, I'd be happy to repeat some things as we drive home today."

Tara closed her eyes and shuddered as Mel snickered beside her. She knew that Will Hester talked a big game but, in the end, was as soft hearted as everyone else at the table. Still, watching him flirt with her great-aunt was disturbing. She suddenly felt the need for something stronger than coffee. Too bad she was in a church. All the wine there was probably consecrated, and she didn't particularly want Jesus involved in the conversation, either.

"You will not be driving me anywhere, you dirty old man. I don't know what's gotten in to the men in this town. Your wives died, and suddenly, you think you're twenty again."

Alma snorted. "I blame it on those blue pills. Pop a few and suddenly they are all wrinkled Casanovas."

Will's smile was lazy as he leaned back in his chair. "You won't find those blue pills in my cabinets, I assure you."

Lady looked at him slyly. "Then I'm definitely not going home with you."

The entire room erupted in laughter, including Will, proving he was as full of shit as Brandon always said. Still, she had a soft spot for the man. Tara's grandfather had been a regular among the men at the co-op. She didn't know what went on when she wasn't there, but when she accompanied her grandfather, the other growers and builders were kind and welcoming. Willie always had gum, and Dale would be quick with a lame joke, never failing to make her smile. After her grandfather died, several of his friends pitched in and made sure her gram and the farm were taken care of. While remembering the lack of concern her mother had shown, it was too easy to forget that there were a great many who did care.

Her mind drifted back to Marley and that look of controlled concentration in her eyes as she focused on her ornament. Tara understood now why Justin was uncomfortable with Marley's silence. She seemed to hide so much behind her lack of words. As Tara pondered this, laughter continued to surround her.

"Well, now, it's nice to see you are all in good moods. Did I miss a joke?"

Father Alex walked in, carrying a plate of donuts and a smile that could warm the entire valley. Mel was the only Catholic among them, but everyone at the table looked a little guilty in the presence of the jovial priest.

"No joke, Father, just the banter of old friends," Will answered for everybody.

"Well, I am happy to hear it. Shall we start with a prayer?"

Father Alex thanked God for giving them the opportunity to serve the community and asked for continued good health and blessings for everyone present before closing with an Our Father, his Argentinian accent bringing a poetic feel to his words. When he was finished, everyone was focused and productive. Within an hour, a schedule was in place, and each member of the small committee had an assigned task and a group of volunteers to oversee. As everyone was saying goodbye and getting ready to leave, Father Alex pulled Tara aside.

"Could I bother you for a moment, Tara? I've been working on something, and I'd like to get your opinion."

"Of course, Father."

Tara was not one of his parishioners, but she had interacted with the priest many times in the past few years. She knew that he was raised in Argentina and had been a truck driver there before immigrating to America and entering seminary. She also knew he was a gifted painter and would sell his artwork from time to time to benefit the parish.

"I knew you would be here, so I brought this

over from the rectory. I've been working on it for a month, and I think I almost have it."

They had entered his small office, and Tara's eyes were immediately drawn to a large canvas leaning against the far wall. It was abstract, as all of his paintings were, with dark colors and almost violent strokes creating streaks and waves. The subject was pain, and the emotion of the piece made Tara's breath catch.

Father Alex squeezed her elbow. "Good. Maybe it is finished."

"I wasn't expecting to see something so dark. It's not like your usual work."

"Oh, there are plenty of pieces like this in my mother's home. She kept everything I did when I was younger, before I found some hard-earned peace."

She turned to him. "Are you not at peace now?"

He smiled kindly. "Perfectly so, but that does not mean the pain does not exist, is not integrated in there somehow."

Tara smiled. It was always odd, yet comforting, to see clergy as human. "Aren't we supposed to pray the pain away?"

He nodded. "Yes. We give it up to God, and sometimes he gives it back to us so that we can create something like this so that someone else can see it and feel what they need to feel. Then they can give up their own darkness, help someone else, and so on. Our gifts are not our own, Tara. We can use them selfishly, hide behind them, or we can have the courage to go as deep as we need to, even when it hurts like hell."

The curse didn't surprise her, but the look on his face did. It was both warm and challenging, as if he knew something she did not. Uncomfortable, she turned her gaze back to the painting.

"Will you give this one to Joe at the gallery?"

"If he thinks he can sell it."

"I don't think he'll have any trouble. It's beautiful work. Thank you for showing it to me."

"Thank you for taking a look. Your reaction was what I had hoped it would be. The opinions of fellow artists mean so much." He guided her out of his office and through the hall. "I'll see you at Thanksgiving if not before."

She nodded and mumbled, "Have a great day," as she made her way down the steps.

Driving the short distance up the hill to her house, Tara suddenly felt like a hack—a hypocritical hack. She had judged Charlotte's clients harshly for being shallow and focused on the wrong things. Seeing the rawness of Father Alex's painting made her feel as shallow and phony as the bland woman in the video Charlotte had shown them.

Tara pulled into her driveway and grabbed her box of supplies and walked to her studio. Her clay work and landscapes were nice. They showcased her skill and the love she felt for her town. But when had she ever put herself on the line to create something that truly had meaning and not just beauty? Art moved her, deeply, so why had she not expressed that depth in her own work?

The image of Marley's hooded eyes focused on the representation of the farm pushed itself to the front of her mind. She let out a shaky breath and stood there for a moment. Her butt wasn't in the seat, but the damn muse was there and was going to have its way, whether she was ready or not. Tara walked across her small space and looked down at her potter's wheel. She pushed the heavy piece to the side to make room for her easel. She pulled a canvas from the closet and gathered paints—acrylics instead of watercolors.

For years she had focused on the beauty of nature. Leaves, plants, and mountains were her favorite subjects. They made her happy and brought enjoyment to those who looked at them. This time, however, as she stroked the canvas with her brush, the beauty of nature was not represented. Instead, her strokes created a fierce and violent storm.

Chapter Twelve

Tara stood in the middle of a giant furniture warehouse that was located off the highway between Sylvan Hills and Asheville and waved off the attention of the overeager sales girl—again. Tara wasn't sure if it was the potential sale or the way Justin filled his jeans that kept the girl coming back. She really couldn't blame her either way. As expected, Justin said yes to everything Marley wanted, racking up a sizeable bill in the process. The way he doted on his little sister only added to the large amount of sex appeal he already possessed in those jeans and a long-sleeved T-shirt that showed the definition of his broad shoulders and arms. Nope, she didn't blame the girl at all.

Marley had long since picked out a lovely set of bedroom furniture and a funky side chair for her room along with rugs and wall prints and was now sitting with her phone in the customer lounge while Justin took his time looking at things for the rest of the house. He came well prepared with measurements and was methodical in his selections. They had been there all morning, and he had picked out one lamp.

Now he was hovering around a dining table that looked like a prop from *Game of Thrones*. It had wolves' heads carved on the legs and was obviously meant to go home with a vacation house owner who thought they knew what Native American art looked like.

Tara shook her head. "Your sister is right. You have the absolute worst taste in furniture."

"What's wrong with it?" He honestly looked surprised, as if it weren't the ugliest thing ever carved out of a piece of wood.

"It's huge and far too ornate for a simple farmhouse dining room." She smiled, feeling mischievous. "But, I get it. I grew up with plenty of boys who drove oversized trucks. I know what this is about. There's only one reason a man would buy such a large piece of furniture for two people to use."

He raised his eyebrows in question. "You going to enlighten me, Tara?"

Her smile grew. "Mmm-hmm. It's typical over compensation."

He laughed. "I don't think a guy would ever compensate for anything by buying furniture." He leaned the palms of his hands on the table and smiled, causing a series of thuds to sound in Tara's ears. "But why don't you come closer so we can test that theory."

Tara felt the heat rise in her cheeks. This man

always managed to discombobulate her, even when she thought she was getting the upper hand in the conversation. Justin was a nice guy, clean cut and masculine in a non-threatening way. Every now and then, though, something deliciously wicked came through that all-American goodness, making Tara's insides squirm and fueling her desire to do something equally wicked in return.

Justin laughed at her discomfort and walked around the table to her, placed an arm around her waist, and pulled her into a brief hug. He had been openly affectionate with her that morning, and though he never pushed things far, Tara was becoming used to the feel of him.

"Come on, then. Point me in the right direction. Marley is insisting on us making Thanksgiving dinner this year, and we need a bigger table than the one we have in the kitchen."

"Will this be your first time?"

"Yes, for both of us." He paused a moment and then looked at her. "You should join us. Maybe you can help keep us from making a mess of things. And Marley talks more when you're around. It's nice."

Tara looked away. "You don't need a buffer, Justin. You and Marley are doing great. Probably even better than you realize."

He traced his fingers down her arm. "Then come just because we want you there."

Swallowing hard, she forced her eyes to meet his. It was a genuine offer. The least she could do was look at him when she rejected it. His eyes were so earnest and full of anticipation that she almost felt guilty over her relief of having a legitimate excuse.

"I'm on the planning committee for the annual community Thanksgiving dinner. I'll be working there for most of the day."

He nodded and kept lightly stroking her arm. "You should still come some other time. I think it would help to see that we're not destroying the place, that we're taking great care to leave most things alone, only fixing what's absolutely broken or no longer useful. I'd love to hear your opinion on things."

"You're getting my opinion on your furniture choices. Isn't that enough?"

Tara walked toward a simple country-style set with an oak-topped table and muted colored chairs in various hues. It should be quirky enough for Marley and functional enough for Justin. It would replace the vintage set that had been there before, the one her grandparents bought second hand when they got married. Her Thanksgivings had been spent at that table. The set was in someone else's home now, or perhaps Fran just threw it away. Tara would never know.

Tara wrapped her arms around her stomach. She was too quick to agree to this shopping trip and to everything else. Her interest in him wasn't waning with familiarity. The physical attraction she could handle. But he was firmly settled in a place she couldn't go, where she

117

no longer belonged, and no amount of carnal longing was going to change that.

She felt Justin come up behind her. "It is enough, but I can't promise that I'll stop asking. Brandon's the only friend we've had there so far, and his conversation often only comes in grunts and single syllables."

Tara laughed and relaxed a little, grateful for his attempt to lighten the mood. She gestured to the table. "What do you think of this one?"

He nodded. "It's good. Let's take the tag to the counter."

Tara cocked her head to the side. "That easy? You took an hour to decide on a lamp shade."

He looked down on her with narrowed eyes. "You probably think that's ugly too, don't you?"

"If I say yes will we have to skip lunch while you pick out another one?"

"It's entirely possible."

"It's a beautiful shade. The most perfect lamp shade in the history of electrical lighting."

He smiled and took her hand. "We'd better feed you before our next stop, or there's no telling what we'll go home with."

Tara smiled. They were now back in a safe zone where they could flirt and have fun without the pressure of her disappointments weighing on them. Tara was relieved. Justin, though, was disappointed. She could tell the slight difference in his tone and demeanor, and she suspected he was creating a distance for her benefit alone. His patience and thoughtfulness made it all so much harder.

Chapter Thirteen

Justin stood at his back door, sipping his black coffee, watching the wind attempt to free the last vestiges of a spectacular autumn from their branches. The trees along the edge of the mountain stubbornly clung to their browning leaves even though their neighbors higher up had relinquished theirs weeks ago. The cold air signaled the change of the season that always came long before the calendar declared it, but the leaves would not yet surrender. Justin admired them. Why should they submit to December when November had been so lovely?

Behind him the scents of Thanksgiving were beginning to rise from the various concoctions he and his sister had risen early to create. The old house, with all its drafts and signs of renovations, felt like home that morning. Marley seemed content and almost happy as she concentrated on the holiday and creating all the little touches that she added to the kitchen to mark the occasion. Justin was almost as content and would have been fully content if they could've added one more person to their small party.

Tara had become a regular part of their lives. Justin knew it could not have been easy to help Marley outfit a space that had once been so important to her, but Tara did, not only with the light fixtures, but with various other items in the weeks following their day in Dillsboro. She would show him pieces in the store on the days she was working, and he would bring lunch, and the three of them went on more than one excursion searching for the right furniture. With each day spent together, the space between them diminished, their touches became more deliberate and lingering, and his longing for her became an intense ache that he could swear was reflected in her own behavior at times.

He knew she had been working. She confided in him that she was painting new subjects and that the change both excited and terrified her. Whatever she was painting had her worked up and open, and her excitement drew him to her even more, and she could not hide the fact that she was beginning to feel the same. It shown in her eyes when they were together.

But every invitation to come and view the space she was helping to create was declined, and even with the growing intimacy between them, there was still a wall he had not been able to scale. He was falling for a woman clinging to the past as stubbornly as the leaves on the trees, and he was becoming as restless as the wind.

Justin moved from the door and back into the kitchen, where he set down his mug and pushed up his sleeves. Surely restlessness could be cured by rolling out dough or whatever task Marley put him on. She was standing at the counter, struggling with the food chopper they had picked up in town the other day. Neither of them was comfortable with knives. They weren't comfortable with the oven either, yet there was a large turkey currently roasting in it, proving they weren't entirely in over their heads.

"You want me to do that?"

Marley moved out of the way. "I think the onion is too big. Maybe I should have cut it in half."

"Maybe," Justin croaked out as he pushed hard on the handle. "Or maybe this thing isn't as easy to use as the box suggests." The onion gave way to the blades, and Justin stepped back. "When in doubt, blame the tools, right?"

Marley smiled as she poured the onions into a bowl of bread cubes. "We're going to have to wait until the turkey comes out to put everything else in. I don't think we worked out the timing all that well."

Looking at the clock on the wall, Justin scratched the back of his head. Marley had several dishes ready to go, and the turkey had only been in an hour. According to the instructions they found online, it would need at least three. "I guess we could turn up the oven. If the turkey cooks faster, we can get everything in and eat while it's still Thanksgiving."

Marley looked skeptical but shrugged. "Okay."

Justin turned the dial on the oven and then moved back to the counter. "Now what do you want me to do?"

"Help me tidy up. It's starting to get out of control in here."

Justin smiled and reached for a dishcloth to wipe down the counters. In the hours they had been working on the meal, he learned much about his sister. When they first started cooking, she was the cool, silent creature she always was, methodically following directions and seeming to find confidence in order. As they progressed and the mess, mostly made by Justin, increased, so did her anxiousness that everything go well. He never would have guessed she was a neat freak, but there it was.

She was also a highly creative being. That was something he should have already understood given she was raised among artists. She had gathered pinecones from around the property and scented them with the same fragrance he found in the soaps in his closet. He would have assumed they should smell like cinnamon, but what did he know. She also tied leaves and greenery into decorative garlands and placed them along the cabinets and tables. This was their first holiday as a family, and it touched him that she was trying to make it special.

He reached over and ruffled her hair. She looked confused for a moment, but she smiled and handed him a roll of sausage before grabbing two apples from the fruit basket. "Can you cook the sausage while I try to chop the apples?"

"Okay, just don't cut off a thumb. Nothing ruins a holiday like a trip to the emergency room."

She started to smile but then paled and pointed behind him. "Um, what about a visit from the fire department?"

"What?" Justin smelled smoke and quickly turned to the stove. "Shit!"

He opened the oven door, and smoke billowed out followed by sparks from the top coil. He turned off the oven, pulled out the turkey, and quickly closed the door again. Smoke had filled the kitchen, surrounding the sister whose content expression had disappeared, replaced by a look of abject disappointment. It broke his heart.

"Hey, kiddo. It's okay. It's just a turkey."

She looked helpless as she raised her arms.

"It's everything."

Justin looked around at the dressing, sweet potatoes, and rolls that sat waiting on the counter. They couldn't cook a meal in an oven that shot sparks. He put his arm around her, and surprisingly, she didn't pull away.

"No, it's not. We'll still have Thanksgiving. Just not here. I'm disappointed, too, but there's always next year. By then we'll have a new kitchen with a stove that won't catch fire."

That must have been the right thing to say because she nodded and moved to clear the counter. He stopped her.

"Don't worry about that right now. Just put things back in the fridge while I unplug the stove and open a window. Then we'll go somewhere where the turkey was meant to be smoked."

Marley nodded again and went to her task, still looking as if someone had just kicked her dog.

*   *   *

"Well, what's the damage?"

Tara pulled off her apron and checked her dress for signs of prep work gone astray. She and Shelby, along with a dozen other minions, had labored under their aunt's supervision as they prepared the community Thanksgiving dinner. Most of the dishes had been delivered by local volunteers from the various churches in the community either the night before or that morning, so the majority of the work had been setting up tables and warming food. Still, Tara knew she must be a mess.

Shelby, still perfectly put together in spite of the morning's toil, looked her over from head to toe. "Not a crumb on you. That dress looks great, by the way. I'm surprised you dressed up."

Tara shrugged. "I didn't know when else I'd wear it."

That was a lie. Tara had bought the rust-colored sweater dress specifically for Thanksgiving. Even knowing that Marley and Justin were working hard on their own meal, she harbored hopes of seeing them, seeing *him*. That would require her driving out to the farm, however, and she still wasn't ready to see it in the hands of somebody else, even someone who deserved it.

Justin. The thought of him came on like a breathless sigh. November always brought change to the valley as nature prepared to switch seasons. This year was no different, except she had spent much of it with him, and the slight melancholy she would normally feel once all the leaves had fallen never came. Her work had a lot to do with that, but she wouldn't deny Justin's role.

He was not so firmly lodged in the friend zone as she would have liked. Tara never pulled away when he touched her or when he said her name with such tenderness it made her ache all the way to her toes. Her time with Justin and Marley was special to her, and a big part of her wanted more of it.

Still, now that she could drive to the farm and be with them, pinpricks formed on her neck. She knew the feeling. It was the same one that came from standing in front of a blank canvas too long—blocked and unsure how to move forward, no matter how much she wanted to. So instead of grabbing her purse and keys, she hung up her apron and turned back to her sister.

"Are you ready to eat? I think I heard Father Alex finish with the blessing."

"Yeah, let's go. Aunt Lady is out there making the rounds, and Charlotte and Brandon have probably already made it through the line."

They pushed through the swinging doors of the kitchen into the gathering hall just as two weary-looking figures finished shaking hands with the priest. Butterflies shot through her, immediately being tempered by the dejected look on Justin's and Marley's faces. She walked to them.

"What happened?"

Justin grimaced as he shoved his hands in his pockets. "Apparently, Thanksgiving is the wrong time to test out an old oven."

Standing beside her, Shelby gasped. "You've been there for almost two months, and you haven't used the oven?"

Both Justin and Marley looked down. "We've barely mastered the stovetop. We have gotten really good at hot dogs and mac and cheese, though."

Shelby placed her hand over her heart. The future Pinterest mom in her obviously could not bear the thought of a child eating boxed mac and cheese more than once a year. She put her arm around Marley.

"Come on, sweetie. We have loads of food to choose from." She started to lead Marley away. "We'll save you guys seats."

Thankfully, Justin seemed more amused than offended by Shelby's look of horror. "I'm glad you told me about this, otherwise I think our only option would have been the casino buffet."

"I'm sorry." She genuinely was, knowing how

much it had meant to them. She was also glad she could spend the day with him and still be a coward. Being with Justin felt good, and after all the time she was spending in front of the canvas, allowing inspiration to draw from places she had no desire to go, Tara needed this feeling. The shock of seeing them there gave way to the butterflies. Determined not to think about it too much, she rose on her toes and wrapped her arms around his neck. "I'm glad you're here, though."

She felt him sigh as his arms came around her waist. "I missed you the last few days."

Her grip tightened as he pulled her closer. His hands rested low on her back, and she felt his warm breath on her neck just before his lips grazed her there. It was a slight motion, but it was enough to send a jolt of sensation right through her. His mouth moved from her neck to her ear.

"Do you have any idea how you look in that dress? I haven't seen the inside of a confessional since my confirmation. If I don't let you go now, Father over there is likely to drag me into one by my ear."

Tara let out a small, shaky laugh as Justin pulled back. Thankfully, he left one arm around her as they moved to the line at the food tables. That slight contact had left her wobbly.

"This isn't going away, you know, this thing between us."

She looked up at him as he handed her a

plate as casually as he had just said those words. Those very true words. "No, it's not."

"So we might as well make a go of it, a real, honest effort to get past whatever we need to and see where we can go. We can take it slow, Tara, make sure no one gets hurt."

She swallowed and kept her eyes on him as he led her down the line. His voice had seemed to hypnotize her, and though his tone was casual, his eyes spoke of his seriousness. It took a moment to find the words. "I want to—"

That must have been enough of a confirmation because before the "but" she had been forming could sound, he leaned down and kissed her cheek, a bit farther over than the ones he had given her before, but still not far enough. He then leaned over and kissed the other side. What should have been completely innocent sent her blood boiling as she felt the skin of his cheek softly graze against hers. She was lost to the feeling of him and desperately wanted to go in for more, just not in front of the mashed potatoes.

"Do you think the priest saw us?"

The mischievous glint in Justin's eyes made her laugh through the shock of longing that pulsed through her. It had barely been more than a peck, but it was enough to make her want more, which, she believed, was the whole point. She couldn't be mad at him, though. He had proven it well.

"I think you're safe." Still within the confines

of his arm, she set her plate down and turned slightly, grazing against him as she reached for a roll. His grip on her waist tightened, and she felt far more wicked than she should considering the block that was still firmly rooted. Apparently, she was becoming comfortable with the contradiction. She looked up at him, pleased to see she had thrown him off kilter for once. "At least for now."

Chapter Fourteen

"You are evil." Justin squeezed her one more time before releasing her.

She laughed as she spooned dressing onto her plate. "You started it."

"No, sweetheart. You started it the first time you smiled at me."

Tara was too busy swooning to make a proper comeback, so she just bumped her shoulder against his arm. "Fill your plate so we can eat. I've been smelling this all morning, and I'm starving."

"This is a lot of food."

Tara nodded. "St. Mary's is hosting this year, but several of the local churches contribute either monetarily or through food donations."

"My cousin organizes volunteers for a soup kitchen during the holidays. There are a lot of people involved, but it's nothing like this."

"They try to make it more of a community event rather than a charity. We see people who have no family to celebrate with or those who do but couldn't be with them for whatever reason, as well as those who could not afford the meal. Shelby, Charlotte, and I have been helping every year since our parents got married."

"Avoiding family?"

"Yep, though they will show up eventually. Tom and Fran never miss a photo op."

They reached the table where Shelby had saved seats for them on the end. Brandon and Charlotte were across from them, and Marley was sandwiched between Shelby and Aunt Lady. Tara watched Justin catch his sister's eye with a questioning smile. The smile she gave him in return seemed genuine. Justin must have thought so, too, because he turned to Brandon.

"I assume I have you to thank for the enormous tree that was on my porch this morning."

Brandon shrugged. "I was cutting another one down and thought I'd save you and the runt the trouble."

"Well, the runt and I appreciate it. It's a good thing we started widening the doorways, otherwise I don't think it would fit." He looked at Tara. "Speaking of the doors, Marley thought you might like to have all the old hardware? I understand some of it is at least fifty years old."

Surprised by the offer, again stated so casually, Tara looked at Marley, who seemed as nervous as she had when making the soaps.

"I went to a children's museum once, and in the toddler area, they had old doors laying on their sides with knobs and locks drilled into them. The little kids loved to latch and unlatch the locks and spin the knobs. It was a toy but still really pretty. I know you do clay and stuff, but maybe you could do something with them."

Tara thought she might cry. She did not know for sure if Justin knew what the offer meant to her, but Marley did. It was clear in the worried tone of her voice. The two of them had to stop knocking her to the ground like this.

"My grandfather installed many of those when he inherited the farm. I would like to have them. Thank you."

"You expect the mayor to be here?"

She was a bit jarred by the change of subject. She looked around and realized her family had been staring at her. She felt Justin squeeze her knee. He did know. "Mmm-hmm, why?"

"I've been trying to get an appointment with him. I want to talk to him about the buildings he owns downtown."

"You trying to take over the whole town, Justin?" Tara teased.

He smiled. "No, just trying to guarantee access for the whole town as well as any visitors. Several buildings, including the ones he owns and rents out, do not have wheelchair access."

"So, it's a lawyer thing. Aren't those buildings historic and exempt from having to make changes like that?"

"It's a concerned citizen thing, and no, they are not. Your step-father made extensive renovations to those building and should have provided access then but didn't. He's clearly breaking the law."

He must have just remembered that Charlotte was sitting with them. He looked at her ruefully. "Sorry, Charlotte."

She shook her head. "Don't be. For all he's become since he remarried, he's still a lawyer with a good sense of the law. If he broke it, he probably knew well what he was doing."

Tara thought for a moment about the buildings Justin was talking about. Before the renovations, they had been ordinary, brick-faced facades. Tom added features to make them seem older and, hopefully, more appealing to tourists. Tourists those businesses counted on. Tara didn't know what was involved in creating access but assumed ramps or lifts would take away from the historic appearance.

"If you pursue this, the shop owners who rent those building will likely be angry and possibly even move their businesses. They rent downtown for the historic appeal. Major renovations could change that."

"If we use that as an excuse to deny access, then we haven't learned anything from history. It's discrimination, and the mayor is sanctioning it."

"He's right, my dear." Lady joined the discussion. "My brilliant contractor informed me I was not in compliance a few years ago when I took down an interior wall and added the public bathroom to the store. It didn't take much more effort or money, but if Brandon hadn't told me what needed to be done, I wouldn't have known. Code enforcement isn't what it should be."

133

They all turned to Brandon, who ignored them in favor of his pie. Tara did the same for a moment and then realized that Justin had noticed all this when he was first in town.

"Is that why you won't eat at Proud Larry's?"

He nodded as he took a fork full of turkey. "I refuse to patronize businesses that discriminate. They might as well hang a sign that says people with disabilities not welcome. This country was supposed to be done with that sort of thing half a century ago."

She was surprised by the hard determination of his voice. So far, he had only used that tone in relation to Marley. "Is this what you did in New York?"

"Not for work. My cousin Ann is a wheelchair user, and she used to drag me to all sorts of advocacy meetings. I guess I paid attention. Plus, it's the law. I suppose my training makes me a bit of a stickler."

He had talked about Ann, but never once had he mentioned a wheelchair. "And she's why you are tearing out doorways?"

"She's my best friend. I want her to have access to my home. And, she's pregnant. Her rug rat will need a place to visit in the country. I've already told her I'll have him or her on the tractor as soon as possible. Of course, I'll have to learn how to drive it, first. After I buy one."

The chorus of chuckles that sounded through their small group was interrupted by a much less pleasant sound. Tara did not have time to process everything Justin had said before she had to deal with the one part of living in Sylvan Hills that she hated.

"Well. Here you all are. Tom and I have been here a full ten minutes, and none of you have come to greet us."

Fran McNair Crowley Jackson had arrived and, as usual, sucked all levels of enjoyment from the room. She stood there for a moment in her fashionable political wife suit, looking very much like an older, less motherly version of Shelby. When no one greeted her, she continued her saccharine-laced effusions.

"Charlotte, dear, your father is waiting with the photographer. We've already gotten several shots with Father Alex, but they want some with you as well."

Charlotte and Brandon rose from the table almost simultaneously. "Sorry to disappoint them, Fran, but we're on clean-up duty. If they want a picture of me hauling trash to the dumpster, then send them on back."

Brandon shot Fran a scathing look as he placed his arm around Charlotte's shoulders and led her out of the room. For someone as honest and forthright as Brandon, being around a narcissistic manipulator was never easy. He had a special kind of hatred for Fran, however, knowing how much her very existence had hurt Charlotte.

"Well, Tara, Shelby, I guess that just leaves you two. We have to have some family shots for the paper. The citizens need to know that we are all here supporting the community."

"They already know who was here supporting and who was here for pictures. You don't really want to document that, Fran."

Tara's mother leveled a Brandon-worthy glare on her but composed herself quickly as she looked around their table.

"I see you have some new friends with you. I suppose I can forgive you for not wanting to leave such company."

Seeing the predatory look in Fran's eyes, Tara finally stood. Justin was just the type of man Fran would try to get her claws into—young, rich, and good looking. But Marley's vulnerability was what Fran would feed on if allowed. She needed to feel important and be admired, and needy children were easy to manipulate into giving her the kind of attention she craved. At least until she tired of them and turned cruel or just left. Tara had not been pretty or sweet natured enough to gain Fran's attention, but Shelby had not been so lucky. True to form, Fran looked around Tara to Marley.

"What's your name, sweetie?"

Tara interrupted. "You have citizens to greet, don't you, Fran? She can't vote, so she's of no use to you."

"It's Marley."

Tara looked around to see that Marley's usual bewildered look was hidden behind one of complete awareness. She didn't need Tara's protection. She could see right through the harpy speaking to her. Tara realized she should not have been surprised. Marley had been raised in a multi-layerd city filled with a variety of personalities and backgrounds. Her mother's artist lifestyle likely drew from an even more diverse crowd. Tara was surprised Justin had not intervened. He was likely as intrigued by this new version of his sister as she was.

"That's a pretty name. Is it short for something?"

"Marlena. My mother was an actress."

"And she named you after Marlene Deitrich. I can see why. You certainly have the charm of an old Hollywood glamour girl."

"Not Marlene, Marlena, after her favorite soap opera character. So I'm not as charming as I look."

Shelby, who had been looking on with amusement, wrapped her arms around Marley. "You have charm through the roof, sweet girl. Let's go find dessert."

Tara heard Justin's deep, soft laugh as he rose to stand beside her. Tara stiffened in preparation. After being thwarted, Fran would double her efforts to get in Justin's good graces. Justin wrapped an arm around Tara's waist and pressed his lips to her ear.

"Thank you for trying to protect us, sweetheart, but we'll have to deal with your mother sooner or later."

His voice had returned to the laid-back

version of earlier, as if they were not about to do battle with the devil. She looked at him, seeing a glint in his eye, as if he had figured out some great secret and wasn't telling anybody. He kissed her temple then turned to Fran.

"Mrs. Jackson, my name is Justin. Happy Thanksgiving. I had hoped you would be here today."

"Oh?" Fran preened at the attention.

"Yes, I would like to meet your husband, if you would be so kind as to introduce us."

"Of course. Let me get him for you." In a practiced move, Fran caught her husband's eye, signaling him to her side. Tom came like an obedient lap dog. Tara shook her head. He had seemed like a good man when they were children and would gather at Charlotte's place. His sweet nature was mirrored in his wife, Elizabeth. They lived in town, not far from Shelby and Tara before their parents' divorce. When the fights were bad, they escaped to Charlotte's, where her parents would dote on them all as if they were treasures.

Now Tom was as slick a politician as a small town could make, and his relationship with Charlotte was almost non-existent. There must be some weakness in Tom that allowed Fran to manipulate him so easily, but Tara's anger rested firmly with her mother.

"My dear." Tara was glad Charlotte had left and was spared the sight of Tom's complacent smile.

"This young man wanted to meet you. This is Justin—I didn't catch your last name."

Justin removed his hand from Tara's waist and offered it to Tom. "Justin Hunter. I've been calling your office for weeks trying to get an appointment with you."

Tara watched Justin expertly move Tom away from the crowd, not letting him speak until they were out of earshot. She had to admire his poise. Once again, he was all city lawyer, full of authority. He said he didn't have the killer instinct, but he certainly had something.

"I must say, I'm impressed. I didn't think you had it in you."

Tara tore her eyes away from Justin to focus once more on her mother. "What?"

"I've heard his name in town. It looks like you found a way to get the farm after all."

Leave it to Fran to turn what Tara felt for Justin into something conniving and dirty.

"As wrong as ever, Fran. Sleeping your way into the right positions is your domain, not mine."

"And, yet, your new boyfriend has everything you ever wanted."

Tara looked at Justin once more and smiled. "For once, Fran, I think you are right."

Her mother frowned and followed her gaze to where the two men stood talking. She obviously was displeased with what she saw and left to join them without another word. Tara's smile grew. Fran was right to be concerned. Justin was definitely a man you wanted on your side.

* * *

"What's wrong, Tara?"

Justin's warm hand engulfed hers as they walked up the hill from St. Mary's to her house. Shelby had convinced him to leave Marley with her to help pack up left over food to take to homebound parishioners. Justin offered to drive Tara home, but she wanted to walk instead. It was not yet dark and just cold enough to keep them awake after the feast.

"Nothing. I guess I'm always a little out of sorts when I have to deal with Fran."

It wasn't a lie. She avoided her mother as much as possible, but when she did see Fran, too much of the past was brought forward again, picking at wounds that were only half healed.

"Well. Other than your mother and the mess I made of my own turkey, I had a great day. Thank you for including us. Marley was disappointed, but she seemed to enjoy her time with Shelby and Lady."

"I'm glad you were with us."

They had reached her house, and Justin laughed loudly as they walked up the steps. Tara was pleased to see he appreciated their eclectic Thanksgiving decorations of turkeys sitting down to a feast of Pilgrims alongside streaking scarecrows with leaves hiding the more interesting parts.

"Now, I know Shelby isn't responsible for this, so that leaves you or Charlotte."

Tara laughed as he leaned over the deck railing to get a better look. "It's a collective effort. Charlotte came up with the idea, and I painted it. Shelby placed the leaves on the scarecrows. We try to do something different every year. Our Christmas decorations will be a bit tamer since they will be visible from downtown. The leaves are pretty much all gone."

"This view is incredible. I can see why you paint it."

He pushed off the rail and smiled at her, pulling her close just as the wind began to swirl around them.

"What are you doing this weekend?"

"I'm helping Lady in the shop all weekend. Main Street gets hit pretty hard during Black Friday, and the crowds don't usually dissipate much through the weekend. She'll even open for a few hours on Sunday. After I'm off there, I have to help with the decorations here and Shelby's usual gingerbread madness. Don't ask."

"Are you going to be this busy all through the holidays?"

"No. It will slow down by Monday."

"Hmm. I guess this will have to hold me over until then."

Though she had been anticipating it since he took her hand and led her out of the church, the warmth of his kiss still had her reeling. His lips gently caressed hers, slowly drawing out her response as his hands moved from her back to stroke her jaw.

Tara sighed as her own hands roamed in time with his movements. Grateful he had not worn a jacket, she felt every hard muscle of his chest and shoulders beneath her fingers, relishing in the hard strength that his gentle nature disguised.

He tipped her head back to deepen the kiss, and when she opened to his explorations, he groaned, releasing her face to untie the belt of her coat. His arms slipped around her, pulling her against him. Tara straightened her arms at her side, allowing the garment to slide off completely, content with the warmth of his arms around her.

As she wrapped her arms around his neck, the hem of her dress rose, and his hands moved down. Tara trembled when she felt his palms on her thighs and then gasped as he lifted her onto the railing. Her hands left him to clutch the hard wood beneath her.

"Let go, Tara."

His words caused her heart to beat even faster than his kisses. She somehow managed to find the breath to speak. "But I'll fall."

He tightened his arm around her waist and lowered his lips to where they barely touched hers.

"Then we'll fall together."

Chapter Fifteen

Justin had never been shopping on Black Friday. In previous years, he had done all his Christmas shopping online or in quick trips during his lunch hour. This kind of buying frenzy was completely new to him, and it left him with one conclusion: people were freaking nuts.

He and Marley had spent the morning at the local box store picking out a new stove. While there, Justin noticed shelves quickly become bare, ravished by bargain-hunting locusts. He was standing too close to a discounted smoothie maker at one point and was given the stink eye by an old lady until he moved out of the way. She kept her eyes on him as she slowly reached for the appliance and placed it in her overflowing cart, as if she were hypnotizing him out of the desire to grab the thing himself. If Marley had not been with him, he might have done just that, just to see what the woman's reaction would be.

Now he and Marley were at the coffee shop on Main Street, taking a break from the madness and enjoying the smell of pine and peppermint as they sipped their drinks at a small bistro table in the corner. Justin was amazed at the transformation downtown had undergone seemingly overnight. All the decorative turkeys, leaves, and pumpkins had been replaced by garlands and ornaments in the stores and on the street. He had not noticed any Christmas decorations the evening before when he was admiring the view of the town from Tara's deck. A team of elves must have come through spraying Christmas spirit through the streets.

"This is still too hot." Marley sat across from him, blowing on her large mug of hot chocolate. "I'm going to look at their beans. Ann and Garret still grind their own, don't they?"

Justin looked at the long line at the counter. "We can come back when it's not so crowded."

She looked at him as if he were the dumbest thing on the planet. "Whole beans are twenty percent off—today only."

Justin chuckled and reached in his pocket, pulling out his wallet. "Here, take my card. Get a few different bags since they're on sale."

So this was yet another side to his sister—Bargain shopper. No wonder she looked a little too happy in the box store. Justin suddenly felt exhausted knowing he would end up taking her to every shop in town. Hopefully, that would include It's by Nature, if only for a minute or two. He did not want to bother Tara while she was likely swamped with customers, but he did want to see her. The growing warmth in his chest wasn't going to allow too much time to go by without seeing her, touching her, or just being in the room with her.

Justin's mind wandered to the evening before, when her soft body was pressed against his, and he smiled at the memory. It should have been a disastrous day, but being with Tara and her family had made it one of his better holidays. He could tell Marley felt the same way. His smile broadened as he thought about the ways both Tara and Marley had handled Fran Jackson.

Tara was fierce as she stood between them and her mother. Whether it was an act of possession or protection, he wasn't sure, but he'd be happy with either one. When he picked Marley up from helping Shelby, he asked her how she had sized Fran up so well. Marley said she hadn't, she just knew that she had hurt Tara and so must not be a very nice person. Just when he thought neither of those women could knock him further off-balance, they both managed to completely level him.

Stretching his long legs as far as they would go beneath the table, Justin placed his hands behind his head and listened to the soft music playing—someone singing about going home for Christmas. He had no desire to return to New York for the holiday, even if it meant not seeing Ann or Josh on Christmas Eve. It had only been a few months since the move, but Justin felt like he had always lived in Sylvan Hills.

As if the thought of Josh had somehow found its way to his cousin, Justin's phone rang with a familiar ringtone. He didn't even have to look at the screen before answering.

"Josh!"

"Happy Thanksgiving, bro."

"You missed it by a day."

Josh laughed, and Justin could hear various voices in the background.

"You'll have to forgive my tardiness. I was in a country that doesn't celebrate Thanksgiving, while giving a lovely local plenty to be thankful for."

Justin groaned. "How old are you? Didn't we outgrow bragging about conquests about a decade ago?"

"Someone would have to have a conquest before bragging about one, right? Ann tells me you're pining over a woman who doesn't want that heart you keep pinned on your sleeve."

"I live in a town where you get more news from the old men sitting in the barber shop than from the paper, yet you and Ann manage to out gossip them."

Josh laughed loud and long, and Justin smiled. They were as different as two men roughly the same age could be, but they had become good friends in their adulthood. Josh's late mother was Justin's aunt—his mother's older sister. The two women were not close, and Justin and his cousin did not spend much time together until college, when they both worked summers for their grandfather. Eventually, after multiple tragedies hit both sides of his family, Justin, Josh, and Ann had become inseparable. At least until Justin had decided to move away.

"Tell me about this girl and why you haven't been able to seal the deal."

"That conversation with Ann was weeks ago."

"Oh-ho. So you *have* been tangled up in the tinsel."

"I'm not talking about this with you."

"Lighten up, will you. I'm not asking for details. I'm just concerned. You're a decent guy with a few bucks in the bank. You could be an easy target for the wrong sort of girl."

"Sounds like you've been spending too much time with the 'wrong sort of girl.' Tara's not like that."

"Tara, huh? What does she look like? Send me a picture."

Justin pulled the phone from his ear and scrolled through the photos. He had taken one the night before, after their kisses had left her hair messy and lips swollen. No way was Josh getting that one. He swiped a few more times before finding one of Tara and Marley that he had taken at lunch one day. They had both been surprised when he snapped the picture, but it didn't show. Tara just looked beautiful. He tapped on the picture and sent it to Josh.

"Damn. She got any sisters?"

Justin laughed. "Two and you couldn't

handle either of them." Or the giant mountain man who had obviously claimed one as his.

"Such little faith. How serious are you with this girl?"

Justin sighed. He was plenty serious and was just waiting for Tara to catch up. "We're taking things slow."

"And your balls are bluer than the ocean, right?"

"Pretty much."

Josh laughed softly. "Listen, man, I didn't just call to chat. There's been an offer on the company."

"What? I didn't know you were thinking about selling." Their grandfather had left his construction business to Josh and Justin, with Josh, who had always been far more hands on with the company, as the controlling partner.

"I wasn't. But we've never fully recovered since the downturn, and it's just getting to be too much work to turn a profit. For years, I've thought about selling if the right offer came along."

"I had no idea."

"You've had enough on your plate without worrying about this, too. We're not losing money, but it's just too damn much work keeping it afloat. I'd like to start something smaller, something that's my own. Maybe build outside of New York."

Justin was surprised. Josh spent so much time chasing and talking about women that it was sometimes easy to forget that he was actually a good businessman.

"Justin, I know the company is the last remaining link to your mom and her family. Things weren't always good there, but blood is blood."

He almost snorted. No, things were not always good. Most of the time his mother's relationship with her family was strained at best, an absolute nightmare at worst. No one ever seemed to understand or have enough patience with his mother. Not even those who loved her.

"Josh, it's fine. If this is what you want, then I'm on board. I was always the silent partner, anyway."

"Okay. Good. I'll email you the proposal, and we can go from there. So, uh, you coming home for Christmas? I think Garret could use some backup. Your aunt managed to slip her mattress into the guest room when they weren't watching."

Justin laughed just as Marley sat back down, triumphantly carrying a large shopping bag filled with beans. For a moment, his eyes wandered over the faces in the café. Most had become familiar to him in the last months, and it seemed every one of them was smiling happily through the haze of bargain-hunting madness. Marley waved to someone coming trough the door, and Justin noticed the beaded bracelet Tara had made on her wrist. He smiled and allowed the peppermint-scented air to fill his chest. It was Christmastime, and the flavor was finally acceptable. Right on schedule. He rose to order a cup to go.

"No, Josh. I already am home."

Chapter Sixteen

"Ugh, what happened to these lights? They never get this tangled."

Charlotte gave the strand in her hand a good tug, but the knot wouldn't budge. She threw them over the couch and grabbed another set from the box.

"That's because *you* put them away last year. I always wrap them around cardboard," Shelby called from the kitchen, where she was busy attempting to bake the walls of a gingerbread house that she would enter in the contest the town held every year at the downtown tree lighting. Like every other year she had entered, it wasn't going well.

The air in the Crowley-Jackson home was as thick as the eggnog they were drinking. Between the gingerbread, lights, and sugar, the sisters were all on edge.

"Half the decorations are broken. Look." Tara tipped over the box for Charlotte to see. Glass and plastic balls were crushed beneath heavier ceramic pieces. "Did you put these away, too?"

"If we didn't buy such cheap decorations, maybe they wouldn't break so easily. We lose ornaments every year, why are your panties in a twist this time?"

Tara turned away from Charlotte and dropped the box on the floor, likely breaking even more pieces. She didn't care. Her panties *were* in a twist, and it was damned uncomfortable. The constant push and pull she felt over Justin grated on her equilibrium, and she felt as tipsy as if she had consumed the entire gallon of eggnog Shelby had set before them.

The kiss on Thanksgiving had given Justin permission to treat her as something—special. *His* something special. Friday morning, when the store was bursting with customers and Tara thought she would keel over any moment, he arrived with coffee and a sweet, tender kiss that had her spinning as much as the more passionate one the day before.

Saturday, he and Marley convinced her to take a breather long enough to eat soup and bread with them in the breakroom. Convinced the new stove would solve all their culinary woes, Marley showed Tara a recipe she had found for cookie ornaments similar to the clay ones they had made in class. Marley planned to cover their entire tree in homemade decorations. She had looked at Tara with a question in her eyes. Tara braced herself for the invitation to help, but when it didn't come, Tara felt like a troll, knowing that Marely knew it would be futile.

Tara looked at the bare tree in front of her. *That's* what she wanted. Not the cheap ornaments they bought from the dollar store, but the homemade ones she and Shelby had created every year. She wanted her Gram's nativity and the first clay ornament she had created—a wobbly replica of the farmhouse covered in snow, much like the one Marley had made.

She turned back to Charlotte, who had abandoned the lights effort and was now grimacing at her phone.

"You're right. We shouldn't have these ornaments. The ones we should have were carelessly tossed away without thought or feeling, as if they meant nothing to anybody!"

Charlotte didn't answer, just looked at her with no expression, as she always did when she was lost in thought.

"What's wrong with you?" Tara's tone reflected her irritation. Since Charlotte was now reflecting the same expression, Tara chose not to feel guilty.

"I'm giving all my clients notice. I can't do this anymore. Even working for the few that actually care about words and the power of good literature isn't worth being connected with the mediocrity that is pouring from the rest. I'd rather have a desk job where at least no one is pretending to be more than what they are."

The sound of a sheet pan crashing to the floor sent both their gazes toward the kitchen. Shelby stood there with her hands on her hips, her red apron covered in flour, looking very much like Mrs. Claus about to take a group of naughty elves to task.

"The two of you are annoying as hell. Charlotte, you're tired of associating with mediocrity, then stop. Finish your own flipping book, and stop criticizing everyone else who has managed to do so. Until you have the guts to put yourself out there to be judged, you just need to shut up."

She turned her angry eyes to Tara.

"And you, dear sister, are just as much of a wimp. There's this wonderful man who gave up his whole life to raise his sister—a little girl who is probably as lost as we were when we started living on that farm. Only a good man would do something like that. How many of them have we known? And he wants *you*, but you can't get your head out of the past long enough to take a chance with him. Stop dwelling on our childhood! Are you going to give up what could be a good future because you can't deal with the past in an open, honest way? You are just using your hopes for the farm as an excuse, and you know it. And back to you."

Charlotte moved back a step.

"Don't even get me started about Brandon. You both have the chance to be happy, but you're too chicken shit to take it."

Charlotte found her courage and followed Shelby, who had turned back into the kitchen. "Yeah, well, your walls are crooked."

Shelby whipped back around. "Yep, they sure are. And the windows are foggy, and half the tiles are upside down, but at least it is all real. I'll be putting that hot mess on display with all its imperfections and my insecurities along with it while the two of you hide behind your abstract bullshit. Start collecting cats, ladies. They can keep you company when the bitterness and regret catch up to you."

Shelby turned on her heels and went back to her baking. Neither sister left behind was brave enough to follow.

"She always gets crazy at Christmas," Charlotte muttered as she left for her room. Tara nodded but stood there and absorbed Shelby's words. Eventually, she picked up the lights Charlotte had left behind, slowly picking at the knots until they gave way, wishing the knot in her chest would dissolve as easily.

* * *

"Justin, can I talk to you?"

"Of course, kiddo. What's up?"

Justin smiled at his sister as she sat in the chair opposite him. They'd had a great weekend in spite of the mishaps of Thanksgiving. They were becoming more comfortable with each other, and Justin felt they had finally made a turn in the right direction. Maybe it was the spirit of the season, but Marley was smiling more and brooding less. He still thought she spent too much time on her phone, but he would save that battle for another time. Right now, things were good, and he felt they deserved for them to stay that way for a while.

Marley pulled her long sweater over her knees and toyed with the hem. He expected her to ask for something outrageous for Christmas, which he would happily grant if he could. What she requested instead sent his stomach straight through the floor.

"I want to stop going to counseling."

Justin blinked, attempting to calm the panic rising in him, or least not let it show. He'd heard similar words before.

"Why do you want to stop going? Do you not like Maggie?"

Marley shrugged. "She's okay. I just don't think I need to go anymore."

Justin's blood chilled. "I disagree."

She shot him a look so defiant he thought he felt his head snap back.

"This is my life. Shouldn't my opinion matter?"

"You're twelve, Marley. Right now, it's my job to decide what matters. You are staying in counseling."

"Why? I don't need it!"

"Yes, you do, and you might benefit even more if you actually spoke to Maggie."

Her eyes went wide. "You discuss my sessions with her?"

"Very little. Of course, if you'd talk more, she might have more to share with me."

"Shouldn't that tell you I don't need to be there? I have nothing to talk about!"

"It tells me that you *do* still need to be there. You've sorted out nothing."

"How do you know? Can you see into my mind?"

"I wish! Then maybe I could understand why you are self-sabotaging."

"Ah! I am not self-sabotaging, only trying to eliminate something that is a waste of time."

"It's not a waste, and you are not quitting. End of discussion."

Marley balled her hands at her side and made a low grunting sound before screaming, "I hate you!" She turned and stomped from the room as loudly as she could in bare feet.

Justin sat heavily on the couch and ran his hands through his hair. So much for the good-will between them. He ignored the guilt that attempted to rise for being so harsh with her and concentrated instead on the question of why she would no longer want to go to counseling. He had been too relaxed these last weeks and must have missed signs of her waning interest. He would call Maggie in the morning and talk about increasing Marley's sessions from once a week to twice. She obviously needed more time, and Justin would not let her give up. Perhaps the family counselor was the wrong choice. A psychiatrist might be more effective.

His thoughts were interrupted by a chirp on his phone. He picked it up from the coffee table to see that it was an email from Marley's teacher. Assuming it was an announcement about something happening at school, he opened it up.

Justin, I'm sorry to bother you on a Sunday night, but I didn't get a chance to sit down in front of the computer during Thanksgiving. I don't know if Marley has told you, but we had an issue last week with her phone. She was caught twice last week looking at it during class. We have a no tolerance policy when it comes to these things, and I have to ask that she not bring her phone back to school for the rest of the semester. I have spoken to her before about using it at recess. It is allowed, but I fear it is impeding her social progress. I worry about her continuing to use it so much even now that she's made friends. Perhaps you could talk to her. I hope the two of you had a good holiday. Thank you for attending to this.

He threw his phone on the table and rose from the couch. That damn phone. He had no idea she had been using it at school. Justin had thought she was using it to shut him out, but apparently, she was effectively shutting out the rest of the world, too. It had to stop. She could not continue to hide behind a screen. If she didn't deal with reality now, then when it finally came crashing in on her, she wouldn't be able to handle it.

Moving to the stairs with a steely determination, Justin called to her. She didn't answer.

He bypassed the second story, feeling sure he would find her in the attic. He walked through the still doorless entry and immediately saw Marley at the window, looking out with the phone clutched in her hand. She looked small and fragile, miles away from the city-toughened girl who had stopped Fran Jackson in her tracks. The constantly changing personality scared him, and he wished he knew who the real Marely was.

She looked at him as he walked toward her, her face changed as she guarded herself against another fight. He must be a lot easier to read. When he was within arms' reach, he stuck out his hand.

"Give me the phone, Marley."

"What?"

"Don't act surprised. You knew your teacher would tell me about you using it in class."

"So I won't take it to school."

"You won't have it at all. When you are able to behave normally in society, then we can talk about you having it back."

Her eyes narrowed. "'Normally'? What's that supposed to mean?"

"It means you talk—to me, to your counselor, your friends. You can't hide behind that thing forever."

"You can't take it."

Her distraught voice nearly had him faltering. For the first time since they walked together out of the judge's chambers when Justin was granted guardianship, Marley looked like she was going to cry.

He kept his voice and his gaze steady, taking the phone from her hand. "I'm sorry, Marley."

"No, you're not."

She looked at the floor as she walked past him, taking care not to get too close. He could hear her stop on the second floor and enter the room she had been sleeping in. Justin expected to hear a door slam. Instead only the click of the old, rusty knob reached his ears, causing his conscience to ache even more.

Chapter Seventeen

Tara shivered and picked up her mug from the table beside her easel. Her small studio, which had been converted from a detached garage, was always chilly in winter, even with the heat pumping. She had been up all night with Shelby's words ringing in her ears as she painted. Tara knew Shelby was right. She had things she needed to work through, regardless of how hard it might be.

She had started the journey, she now realized, the day she came back from talking to Father Alex. Tara had allowed the pain to take over as she held her brush, expecting to end up with a portrait of her mother. At the end of the day, what she saw instead was the green of her father's eyes set against the backdrop of a swirling tempest.

The impact of it had not hit her, however, until last night when she arranged all her new pieces on the table to view. It happens like that sometimes. The reflection of something hits harder than the actual event. She had not allowed his desertion to affect her in years, or at least that is what she had believed. He had actually destroyed a little piece of her, one that had not begun to grow back until recently.

As she often did when her emotions became too difficult to control, she turned her eyes to the one piece of her own artwork that she displayed on the wall. The watercolor painting was the first rendering she had ever done of the farmhouse. Though it was one of her earlier works, it had always been one of her favorites. It was light and happy and showed the old house in the complete restoration Tara had planned. The painting, and the thought behind it, had always brought her peace. Now, as she stared at it, the image seemed off. There were too many layers.

Tara quickly cleared away the acrylics and set up clean brushes and watercolors. After placing the canvas on her easel, she stared at it for a long while, not quite knowing what to do. Every moment brought more chaos to her thoughts.

She picked up a brush, hoping the movement would calm her. One stroke in, a knock sounded at her door, and she gratefully put the brush back down. Distraction from the whirlwind inside her was welcome. She opened the door to find a disheveled-looking Justin standing there.

"What's wrong?"

He looked toward her easel. "I'm interrupting your work."

She shook her head and pulled him inside.

"Take off your coat and tell me what happened."

He obeyed and sank down into the oversized chair she kept in the corner, looking as helpless as a man his size could. She squeezed in next to him and pulled her feet under her, allowing her knees to cross his lap, instinctively providing support. He put his arm around her and dropped his head to hers.

"I've made a mess of everything, Tara. I never should have moved Marley here."

She moved her head back so she could see him. "I thought things were better, that she was adjusting."

"I thought so, too. We argued last night and this morning. Badly." He pulled a phone from his pocket. "I took her phone away. Her teacher emailed yesterday and said Marley had been caught with it in class twice this week and asked me to make sure she doesn't bring it back. I've been so frustrated with her and this damn phone for months."

He swiped the screen and tapped on the photo app. "I looked at it this morning after I dropped her off. I don't know what I thought I would find."

He drew a breath and handed her the phone. "There's nothing on here but pictures of her mother. The Google searches are all about her, and her YouTube history is all videos of Sharon's performances. There are no games or questionable content. The only other app is for an e-reader. Look how many books she's down-loaded. I didn't even know she likes to read."

Tara swiped through the photos. Marley's

mother was beautiful. That wasn't surprising given Marley's unique physical qualities. Most of the pictures were of her mother alone, likely taken by Marley. The ones of the two of them together were both breathtaking and heartbreaking. It was clear they loved each other very much.

"I took her away from every memory she has of her mother, and now I've taken this, too. What am I doing, Tara? Why did I think I could raise a little girl who so clearly needs more than I can offer?"

Tara put the phone on the chair arm and wrapped her arms around him. "You love her, Justin, and you are committed to her well-being. What more can anyone offer?"

She felt him shudder, and the hand that had been on her knee trailed up to clinch her waist, bringing her even closer.

"She wants to stop going to counseling. That's what started the argument."

She pulled back and saw the panic in his eyes. "Why does that scare you so much?"

Tara could feel his heart pounding through the thickness of his sweater, and she gently stroked his hair until he finally spoke.

"My mother stopped seeing her therapist, and she stopped taking her medication several times. I didn't know about the last time until it was too late."

It took only a moment to realize what he was saying. "Oh, Justin."

"I had not spoken to her in weeks. I was in

the middle of finals at Penn State and sent my cousin Josh to her apartment to check on her. She didn't answer then or the next day when he tried again. I skipped my last exam and got to the city as quickly as I could, but I was a few hours too late. I knew as soon as I turned the key in the lock. The place was just too still—silent just as she had been."

Tears stung her eyes. So much made sense now. His fears for Marley. The ever-present strand of guilt in his eyes when he looked at his sister. She wanted to tuck him close and make it all go away.

"Your mother was sick?"

He nodded. "I never understood that when I was a kid. All I saw was the mood swings. She could be happy and full of life for weeks. She was the best mom then. So attentive and affectionate. Then she would just crash, as if she was exhausted from keeping it all up. I couldn't see what was wrong."

"How could you? You were a child."

"I was too busy blaming my father for everything. His coldness and his absences. He would get frustrated with her when her moods were erratic and just leave. I tried to make up for it, to be enough, but I never was. And then I got frustrated, too. Instead of staying in the city for college, I moved away. I wanted to live my own life more than I wanted to help her." He blew out a loud breath. "I can't do that again. Not with Marley."

He blamed himself. That was perfectly clear, even though he was as much of a victim of the situation as his mother had been. This impossibly kind and fiercely protective man felt he had failed and was terrified of it happening again.

"You're afraid Marley's depressed, too?"

"I don't know how else to explain her behavior. Her counselors have both said she doesn't open up to them the way they would like. She never talks to me unless it's to argue. She spends too much time alone, and I honestly don't know what version of her is going to be sitting across from me at the dinner table."

"Justin," She took his face in her hands. "That doesn't mean she's ill. She's grieving and *she's twelve*. If you give her enough room, she will eventually feel comfortable enough to talk to you. But you can't let your own fears suffocate her."

"Is that what I'm doing?"

"Maybe." She leaned in and smelled his shirt. "You smell of bergamot and sandalwood."

"Yeah, Marley put soaps in my closet. I'm not sure what she's trying to tell me."

"I helped her make those in her class. She asked me which essential oils were best for relaxation. Those are the ones she chose."

"For me?"

"It seems so. You don't see how tense she gets when she thinks you are upset. Her stance is a nearly perfect reflection of yours. Just learning how to relax around each other would be a huge improvement."

He blew out a long breath and leaned his head against the back of the chair. "I told you I don't know what I'm doing." He closed his eyes and sighed. After a few moments, his breathing steadied, and he repeated Tara's words. "She's grieving and she's twelve."

The affirmation seemed to calm him, but she continued to stroke his face, wanting to provide comfort.

"You know, Shelby and I were in a similar situation as Marley. Abandonment isn't the same, but it can feel a little like death. I think the grieving process is probably similar. We had Gram to provide a safe place for us to heal. You are doing that for Marley. Don't doubt the positive impact you have on her, even when you make mistakes. Most people have years to grow into this parenting thing. You didn't have that luxury, but it's still going to take time, and I know you are never going to give up."

He sighed, hopefully in recognition of that truth. Tara curled into him, and he did not speak for a while, just sat there stroking her hair. Tension eventually eased out of both of them.

"How long did it take you?"

"To what?"

"To grieve?"

Tara thought for a moment and then looked at her easel. This was the truth she had been painting for days but saying it out loud was still difficult. "I honestly don't know if I ever did. I've just held on to the anger, to the pain. I didn't know how it was affecting me until recently. I put all my focus on my plans for the farm, ignoring everything else. Please don't allow yourself or Marley to do that."

Justin didn't look at her, just continued his ministrations. He had come to her for comfort, but he was giving plenty of his own without realizing it. She leaned up and kissed him, hoping to convey what she was feeling even through her own confusion.

Before long, the kiss deepened, and the hand on her waist began to move. She nearly whimpered when he pulled away just slightly, his eyes staring into hers.

"You are so beautiful, Tara, so loving. Don't allow yourself to do that anymore, either."

He kissed her again, moving over her as if he never wanted to stop. Tara surrendered to his touch and nearly drowned in the promise of it.

Chapter Eighteen

Justin tapped his fingers against his thigh as he waited for Marley in the carline at school. He called Brandon and asked him to clear out of the farmhouse for the afternoon. He had a feeling he and his sister would not need an audience for the conversation they needed to have. One look from her as she got in the car told him that conversation wasn't going to come easy.

"How was your day?"

Marley didn't respond. She turned in her seat and looked out the window as he pulled out of the parking lot and onto the street. Nearly every house he drove past was decorated for Christmas. Some were clearly displayed for the enjoyment of children, with colorful lights and cartoon characters. Others were understated and elegant. Justin had never considered himself a Grinch, but he had not shown much Christmas spirit in the past. He was single and alone except for his small circle of family, and Christmas was about tending to others, people you loved. Now that he had Marley and was making slow but incredibly sweet progress with Tara, he wanted it all: the decorations, the food, the music, and, most of all, the magic that came from believing in something bigger than yourself. First, he had to make things right with his sister. He drove a few miles before he tried again.

"Marley, you have to talk to me. I'm sorry I took your phone. I didn't realize until I looked at it why it was so important to you."

She turned to him. "You looked at it?"

"I did. I had to see what was taking your attention from everything else. Marley, I don't think I every told you how sorry I am about your mom. I'm sorry she died, and I'm sorry I never really knew her and didn't know you until this year."

She didn't answer and Justin sighed. "Marley—"

"Just stop, okay. Just stop being so nice to me. Stop trying to take care of me. You don't have to. I know you think you do, but you don't."

They reached the farmhouse, and Justin waited until he parked to respond. "I do have to take care of you. You are my sister."

"Just stop!"

Marley got out of the car and ran through the yard. Surprised by the outburst, it took Justin a moment to follow. He found her at the broken fence between the yard and the pasture, standing still as she looked toward the mountain.

He stepped forward cautiously, fearing she would bolt again if he got too close.

"Marley."

"Shh. Look."

Justin followed her gaze to the edge of the mountain, where a small herd of elk stood grazing. The size of them was magnificent, but their elegance was breathtaking. He stood there with his sister, at least two arm's length between them, and watched as the beasts lowered their heads to the ground. They did not seem frightened but confident that the land belonged to them before anybody else. Before long, a smaller, but no less extraordinary, one broke free from the rest and wandered slightly away from the trees. Soon, he was joined by another, who gently attempted to guide him back to the herd.

Justin heard Marley's sharp inhale and turned to her. Her short breaths turned to puffs around her in the late afternoon air, and her shoulders shook. In that moment, all the walls were down. She was suddenly just a little girl surrounded by grief and wonder as she watched the giant animal gently nudge her young. She breathed in sharply, and he could see the last vestiges of her anger give way to tears—fat, silent drops that fell onto the gloved fingers that she clasped tightly on the fence. He stepped toward her, and she dropped her head.

"*I'm* sorry about *your* mother."

"Thanks. It was a long time ago, but—"

"No, I'm sorry that she—about how she died. That it was because of me and my mom."

Justin blinked. He shook his head, closed the

distance between them, and put his hand on her shoulders, leaning down until she had no choice but to look at him.

"Where did you get that idea?"

More short puffs came from her as she spoke. "When you were traveling looking for houses and I was staying with Ann, Aunt Linda came by one night. I was doing my homework, but the walls are thin, and I could hear them talking. She told Ann that she hoped I realized how hard keeping me was for you, that your mother probably wouldn't have killed herself if she hadn't found out about us."

Simultaneous feelings of sadness and rage tore through him. His aunt wasn't cruel, but her ignorance certainly made her seem so at times.

"And how did Ann respond?"

"If I repeated it, you probably wouldn't give me back my phone."

Justin nodded. "I wish you would have listened to *her* and not Aunt Linda." He kneeled down until he could look directly in her eyes. "Marley, listen to me. What happened to my mother was not your fault. It was not your mother's fault, or my fault, or even our father's, though God knows I blamed him and myself enough. She was sick and had been for a very long time, probably her whole life. She had access to doctors and medication, but in the end, it was too much. Her death was as biological as cancer, and no one is responsible for it."

It was the truth, and for the first time, Justin

accepted it. He rose and gently pulled Marley to him. She didn't resist, and he could feel her sobs as he rocked her. He felt like he'd been kicked in the chest. The idea that this had been weighing on her for months, along with everything else, killed him.

"Marley, you have to trust me enough to talk to me. I can't take away your grief over losing your mom. That has to run its course. But I could have taken this off you. Guilt puts such a strain on your heart, even when there's no need for it."

"I didn't want to hurt your feelings by bringing it up. You're wound so tight sometimes, and I didn't want to make it worse."

What was he saying about guilt? "I'm sorry, Marley. I think I'll be less wound now. And I'm sorry for freaking out about counseling. You were trying to talk to me, finally, and I completely shut you down. I'll try not to do that again. But after what happened to my mom, it scares me when people get sad."

"Maggie says it's natural to be sad sometimes, even when you're happy."

"Yeah, I get that now. Listen. If Maggie thinks it's okay to stop counseling, then I'm okay with it, too. I would like us to have a couple of sessions together, though, just to work some things out."

She pulled away from him and nodded. "Okay." She looked by toward the mountain. "The elk are gone. They were pretty cool, huh?"

They turned and walked slowly toward the

house. "Yeah, it's like we have our own reindeer. Pretty fitting for the season."

"You know I don't believe in Santa, right?"

"Yeah, I figured." He was a little disappointed. He would like to have experienced that part of her life.

"I could be persuaded, though, if it got me more presents."

Justin laughed. The girl wouldn't have to believe in Santa for him to load the house with gifts on Christmas morning. Marley deserved every good thing he could provide.

Chapter Nineteen

Tara stepped back from the easel and attempted to rub the crick out of her neck. Letting out a yawn, she turned her stiff body toward the clock behind her. It was past 9:30, and she had not given herself a break since dinner, which had consisted of tea and a small bag of chips she had stowed away in one of the cabinets. She sighed as she looked at the canvas. The painting of the farmhouse had once been as perfect as the one in Marley's ornament and as pretty as all the landscapes Tara had painted and sold through the years. What it had not been was honest.

She did not like painting portraits, and only now did she realize why. There was too much potential for truth, and damn, had creating the new, small images on the painting knocked her on her butt. Her heart hammered the entire time, and only when she had stood back to view her progress could she see what she had actually created.

The walls of the house, once pristine white, were now marred with gray streaks and cob webs, much like it had been the last time Tara saw it. A swirling tempest, similar to the one she painted earlier, brewed in the background, threatening and scary. A girl with wild, dark hair ran on the lawn, attempting to get inside while another girl with similar features held on to the hem of her shirt, not letting her move. The wild haired girl reached out with both hands, her face contorted in desperation. The door was cracked, but she couldn't go in. The storm was going to devour her.

It was dark, it was emotional, and it was completely unsellable. Yet, Tara knew she would do more in this vein. Aunt Lady had warned her about letting art take a backseat to money, and apparently, her muse had listened.

Deciding she couldn't take anymore for the night, she set to work cleaning her brushes, only to be interrupted by the sound of her phone. She picked it up and saw the number she had been hoping to see since Justin left that afternoon.

"Hello."

"Hi, sweetheart."

"Justin." She walked across the room and settled into the chair. "I've been thinking about you and Marley all evening. How did it go?"

She heard him blow out a long breath, and she wished she was with him, stroking his hair as she had done that afternoon. "Well, I now know why she never talks about her mom. She doesn't want to make me feel bad because she blames herself and Sharon for my mother's death."

"Oh my God."

"Yeah. Apparently, she overheard a conversation that never should have happened and has been carrying it around with her ever since."

"She knows better now, though, right?"

"We talked about it, and hopefully, I got through to her. Thing is, once you start blaming yourself for something, it's hard to stop."

"Maybe the two of you can work on that together."

"I have a lot I need to work on when it comes to her. Our relationship is as battered as this old house."

"Ah, but that old house has a strong foundation and only needs some attention to make it as beautiful as it ever was." She drew in a deep breath, allowing the truth in with it. Marley needed the farm just as much as Tara ever had. Justin needed it, too. "You did the right thing bringing her here."

"You really believe that?"

"I do."

She heard him sigh again and could imagine a slight smile on his face. "What were you doing when I called?"

"I was just about to call it a night and put my brushes away."

"You're still working? It's almost ten o'clock."

"Artists don't keep regular hours, I'm afraid."

They were silent for a moment, and Tara thought she heard the rustling of sheets, like he was getting into bed. She curled further into the chair, letting the idea of his relaxed, sleepy frame take over her mind. What would he sleep in, she wondered. Shirtless? That was the picture she chose. Having felt the strength of his arms around her, she could only imagine what they would look like bared. She thought back to the first time they met and how she had wanted to sketch him. The thought of that portrait, surprisingly, did not frighten her at all.

"Would you model for me?"

"For a painting?"

"Yes."

He laughed softly, intimately. "If you want to get me naked, Tara, there's an easier way to go about it."

The tone of her laugh mimicked his. "And what would that be?"

"Just get naked first."

She could actually feel herself blushing, though he was miles away and had no idea how hard her heart was beating at the thought. "It's the model who is supposed to bare it all for the artist, not the other way around."

He tisked. "Who knew such double standards existed in the art world. Okay, then. You can model for me."

She smiled, feeling lighter than she had in months. It could be the painting and the emotional deluge that came with it, but Tara suspected it had more to do with the man. "You are wicked, Justin Hunter."

She heard the sheets rustle again. "Sweetheart,

you have no idea." Then after a slight pause he added, "But I can't wait to show you."

Chapter Twenty

"Well, Justin, it seems you and Marley have made great progress the last few days."

Maggie Evans, the family counselor in the lone agency that served the county, looked at him with kind eyes. She was short and round and had a motherly quality to her that made it nearly impossible not to spill your guts. Justin felt like he had done just that in the hour they were supposed to be talking about Marley.

"Yes, I've learned that Marley is a normal kid going through a tough time, and I've made it worse by projecting all my guilt and fears onto her. Does that about sum it up?"

"Not entirely. In all our sessions, Marley never really spoke about anything deeper than what's typical for her age—peer pressure, body image, things like that. Her counselor in Manhattan said the same thing. When she finally opened up, it was to you. What do you think that says?"

Justin shrugged. "That I drove her nuts to the point that she couldn't take it anymore."

"That she trusts you. It says a lot about how far you've come."

Justin allowed that thought to settle for a moment. Tara had said something similar when he told her that he and Marley had talked. "So, do you think she can stop coming to counseling?"

"I think the two of you would benefit from a few joint sessions, but, yes, I think Marley has advanced as much as she is going to from counseling. She's a bright, mature girl. She was never confused about how she felt, only about how you felt. But, please, keep talking to her. There's a delicate balance between pushing too much and giving enough space, but if you keep communicating, you'll find it."

Justin nodded and rose from his seat. "Thank you, Maggie. This helped a lot."

"I'm glad. Be sure to stop at the desk and make an appointment for you and Marley after the holidays. Are you going back to New York for Christmas?"

"No, this is home now."

"Good. Marley does like it here, you know."

Justin smiled. "Thanks again, Maggie. I hope you have a Merry Christmas."

Justin felt great leaving Maggie's office and decided to go downtown and finish his Christmas shopping. Marley had not given him a list, so all he had so far was a gift card to one of the box stores in town and one for online. The bookstore downtown would be his next stop. Marley liked to read on her phone, but it's hard to put an e-book under the tree.

Downtown was brimming with Christmas.

Every shop window was elaborately decorated with fake snow, candy canes, snowmen, and every other symbol of the season. They may not be as ornate or elegant as the ones he knew were currently on display in New York, but they were lovely just the same. At the end of the street, in front of the courthouse where the fountain had previously been, stood a massive Christmas tree. Several smaller trees dotted the courthouse lawn, waiting for the official lighting the next night. Marley's school band would be playing during the festivities, and she was all nervousness and anticipation, as every child should be at Christmas.

As if by habit, his eyes were drawn to the right and up to where he knew Tara's house could be seen. The week before, he would've had to focus a bit more to see it at the right time, but now no focus was needed. In fact, their yard might have even been seen from space. It was the most decorative display he had ever seen, packed into their tiny quarter of an acre yard that was mostly sloped mountain. Something white had been laid on the hill with a large cartoon dog figure on skis pointing down, looking as if he was heading right toward a pyramid of terrified looking penguins several feet below. How the hell had they gotten that set up without falling right down the hill?

The deck was filled with rotating snowmen and candy-striped pillars, and Santa's sleigh, complete with gifts and reindeer, was planted on the roof. Santa himself seemed stuck in the chimney. Justin could only imagine what would light up on the jolly old elf once the sun went down. It was all fantastically hideous and sure to make everyone who looked at it smile.

Justin realized he had been sitting at a green light as he was staring and moved the SUV forward with a jerk. Instead of turning on the street that would lead him to the bookstore, he kept straight and made the turn that would take him up the hill to Tara's. He had to get a close-up view of that exhibition. Getting a close-up view of her would be an added bonus.

He pulled into their driveway, and indeed, it was even better, or worse, depending on your point of view. He smiled again as he made his way from the car to the door. His every interaction with Tara was more and more tender and exciting, and he expected a smile almost as big as his when the door opened. Instead, he saw an exhausted Tara and heard a string of expletives the likes of which had not reached his ears since the days he worked construction with his grandfather.

Tara's eyes went wide. "Justin!" She let him in and turned back toward the kitchen. "Shelby, Justin is here." Her words seemed to contain a plea, and the rant that was still going on became slightly quieter.

"Have I come at a bad time? I can come back later. Or not."

"Oh, please stay. If you are around, perhaps Shelby will check her language."

His eyebrows rose in curious wonder. Shelby had never been anything but serene and composed around him. Just then, another slew of curses sounded from the kitchen. He nodded in appreciation of the creativity of some of them.

"She goes a little crazy at Christmas."

His usually animated girl was so deadpan he could not help but chuckle.

"I'm serious. You are not ready to see this side of my family. She's trying to finish her gingerbread castle for the tree lighting. It isn't going well. Charlotte and I are trying to help, but Shelby doesn't make it easy."

He laughed again and pulled off his jacket, laying it across the back of the couch. "After the other day, I think we can handle a little Christmas drama. How can I help?"

Apparently, that was the right thing to say. The smile he received was better than he anticipated. The kiss that followed was even better. By the time it ended, Justin couldn't feel his toes.

"You are going to regret this."

"Come on. Shelby's the nicest person I've ever met. How bad can it be?"

"Hey! It isn't make-out time. It's gingerbread time. Save it for the mistletoe and get your butts in here. I need someone to hold these walls together."

If Tara looked exhausted, Shelby looked absolutely crazed. He followed obediently, receiving an apologetic look from Charlotte as he entered the kitchen.

"Coffee is over there if you need it, but nothing stronger. I need steady hands. Charlotte's already broken three reindeer."

Any boldness he had ever seen in Charlotte was gone as she cowered in her chair, slowly piping icing onto what seemed to be a ginger princess. He wanted to laugh again but thought it would be wiser to save it until he was at a safe distance.

"I'm good. Where do you want me, Shelby?"

"Can you please help Tara put these walls up while I try to fix Charlotte's mess?"

A flash of defiance appeared in Charlotte's eyes, but it disappeared with one quick look from Shelby. Justin had to bite the inside of his cheek to keep from laughing.

"Where's Brandon?"

Tara gave him a pained look and gave Shelby a sly side eye. "He didn't make it."

He snorted, barely holding it in at the thought of giant Brandon succumbing to gentle Shelby's Christmas insanity.

"If you start laughing, you will never make it out of here alive. Every year she turns from Thanksgiving princess to the witch from *Hansel and Gretel*. One of these years, someone is going to find us in the oven."

Tara's panicked whisper only made it worse, and soon, his whole body was shaking, sending the gingerbread walls tumbling down.

"It was Justin's fault!" Tara had jumped back and was pointing at him as if they were all five years old. He looked at her through narrowed eyes.

"You jumped up eagerly at Thanksgiving to protect me from your mother but throw me under the bus now?"

"Yep! Shelby is *much* scarier than Fran."

One look in Shelby's direction confirmed that statement. It was just too much. The woman was basically a sprite with the sweetest disposition he had ever come across, yet she had two brave, focused women shaking in their boots. He had the brief vision of Brandon hiding somewhere in fear, and he didn't even try to hold back his laughter. Soon, Charlotte joined him. Shelby's glare turned in her direction.

"Oh, Shelby, please don't be mad. We are trying our best. Well, not Justin, he hardly tried at all. But you gotta cool it, sister. You are going to have an aneurism. No one is going to marry you if you have an aneurism over gingerbread."

Even scaredy cat Tara cracked up with that one. Shelby, however, was barely affected by their laughter.

"You are all useless. Justin, can Marley come help after school? She might have better luck piping with her smaller hands."

"No way. Tara thinks you are going to cook her in the oven. If you'd bake your own sister, what would you do to mine?"

Shelby placed her fists on her hips, somehow looking wounded by the implication. "I would never hurt a child."

"Any Christmas witch would say that right before she slams the oven door."

Shelby finally smiled, barely. "I swear I will be on my best behavior. I'm never going to get this done without help. It's already going to be the ugliest one there, but it at least has to be there in one piece. I haven't missed a year since our grandmother died."

Every brotherly instinct rose up in him, and he could do nothing but acquiesce just as he would with Marley. His shoulders slumped as he heard Tara behind him whisper, "Sucker."

"Okay, but it'll be a trade. You can have Marley this evening, but I get Tara this afternoon."

Shelby thought for a moment. "All right take her. Charlotte can finish what Tara started."

Justin ignored the panicked plea in Charlotte's eyes and grabbed Tara's hand, pulling her into the living room.

"Get your coat. Let's get out of here before she changes her mind."

Tara laughed and did as bid. When they were safely outside, she turned to him and snaked her arms around his neck. "Thank you for saving me from the ghost of Christmas crazy. How would you like to be rewarded?"

His look must have been as wolfish as his thoughts since a lovely blush rose in her cheeks. He pushed those thoughts aside for the time being. She had not yet agreed to come to the farm fully clothed. He could not suggest she spend the rest of the day there naked.

"I'd like to hold your hand as we look at all the decorations downtown and, hopefully, finish my Christmas shopping. And you can tell me how you managed to set up the most garish holiday display I've ever seen on the side of a mountain."

She smiled mischievously and pressed even closer. "There's a perfectly reasonable explanation."

"Did you hire a crane or talk Brandon into using some sort of rope contraption?"

"Of course not. There was no need for anything so elaborate."

"Oh?" He could not help but smile at the look in her eyes as she slowly lifted her mouth until it was barely touching his.

"Mmm-hmm. It was all Christmas magic."

He laughed softly and lifted her by the waist and proceeded to show her some magic of his own.

Chapter
Twenty-One

Just as she promised, Shelby behaved herself while Marley patiently helped her finish the piping on all the little gingerbread people that now stood perfectly around the crooked walls of the castle. After picking Marley up from school, they all worked hard to make sure the structure at least stood upright and somewhat resembled the winter wonderland Shelby had envisioned. Even Brandon was brave enough to reappear after Justin called and promised him dinner if he would come help. If one ignored all the other gingerbread creations on the table, this one didn't look half bad.

"Oh my goodness. They all look so pretty." Marley had come to stand beside Tara, holding her clarinet case in her hand. It was almost time for the tree lighting, and Tara looked forward to hearing her play with the band. "Shelby isn't going to win a prize, is she?"

Marley was talking about the contest, but thinking about the night before and how well she and Justin fit with them, Tara knew that she and her sisters had indeed won something worth far more than a medal and bragging rights.

"Probably not, but the experience was priceless."

Marley gave her a sly smile, displaying more of that wicked humor she was getting more comfortable showing. "I better go warm up. Justin is back there somewhere. He got stopped by a bunch of old men asking about trees."

"Okay, I'll see you after the lighting for the judging."

Marley nodded and then shuffled away with the tree skirt she had fastened to her band uniform flowing around her calves. Tara was pleased to see the girl embracing the local traditions. The tree lighting always brought out the craziest outfits, with each citizen trying to out ugly the next. Her own sweater was a wonderful display of tackiness. She had sewn on mini dollar store flamingos, dressed as elves, kissing under the mistletoe. Thankfully, they had been blessed with higher than normal temperatures, so she could show off her creation without freezing from the lack of a coat.

She had just decided to find Justin and free him from the senior crowd when she turned and saw him heading her way, wearing a smile and a poinsettia cardigan any old lady would be proud of. He leaned down and kissed her, careful to not crush her flamingos.

"Hi."

"Hi."

He kissed her again. "Have you seen my sister?"

She smiled. He was trying, but his protective nature was hard to repress. "She's with the rest of the band, warming up."

He looked over to confirm and then smiled down at her. "Come on, let's go get a good spot."

They walked hand in hand to the tree, moving to where they could clearly see Marley sitting in the front row. She gave a little wave when she saw them, and Justin pulled out his phone for pictures. Tara could see Marley roll her eyes, but Justin just laughed and kept clicking.

"You're becoming such a dad."

He honestly looked terrified for a moment, but it was soon gone, replaced by something soft and peaceful.

"There are worse things to be."

Tara felt tears in her eyes. Not wanting him to see, she wrapped her arms around his waist and placed her cheek on his chest. He reciprocated the gesture, resting his chin on the top of her head. She wasn't as good at hiding her reaction as she thought.

"What's wrong?" He pulled back and gazed into her watery eyes.

"Nothing. I'm just proud of you."

"Me? An unemployed former attorney with daddy issues, a crumbling house, and a temperamental twelve-year-old girl?"

"Yep, you. You are fighting against all that to build a good life."

"It's worth fighting for, Tara."

She could see lights reflecting in his eyes and realized that while she had been lost in them, the trees had been lit. She continued to stare at the reflection, finding more wonder in it than anything else around them. She could hear the music playing and felt him shift her to one arm so he could record Marley's solo, never taking his eyes off his sister or his arm off of Tara. They stayed connected that way until the next piece started and his other arm returned to her.

"My father's parents paid my mother to leave town. She dropped us with our grandmother, took the money, and didn't look back until it ran out. My father just ran out."

"I know. Brandon told me."

"Why did I ever think he was a man of few words? His father is also a class-A jerk. There aren't many stand-up men in my family. You might take some getting used to."

He smiled. "We have time. I'm not going anywhere."

The music shifted from festive to a slow and bluesy version of "Jingle Bells." Justin's hands moved to her waist as he pulled her closer, effectively crushing her flamingos against his poinsettias. Her hands found their way around his neck as they began to move in slow circles.

"There's usually not dancing at this event."

"No? Well, when it's a mild night and lights

are twinkling all around, soft music is playing, and a beautiful woman is in your arms, there should definitely be dancing."

Tara relaxed against him, enjoying the music, the motion, and the new sensation of falling in love with a good man. The music stopped and so did Justin, but he did not release her.

"We are going to embarrass your sister."

"Good. She picked out this sweater for me to wear. She deserves a good embarrassment."

"But you fit in so well."

"You think? I still feel like a fish out of water some days."

He turned her around to face the tree and returned his arms to her waist. There would be no decorations, just the beautiful twinkling of strand after strand of clear lights. Tara loved this tradition and was grateful that even in tough economic times, the town still made it a priority.

"You get to see this from your windows every night. I could do that in the city, look out my window and see lights, but they were never this magical. Of course, that could have a lot to do with the company." He kissed the top of her head. "What will I see at the farm?"

"Nothing like this, I'm afraid. But you'll have a beautiful, clear sky, the smell of firewood, wild turkeys, the occasional bear, and, of course, the elk. But he greatest beauty will be inside."

"Marley has certainly been working hard on that. There's not a surface in the house that doesn't have some sort of homemade decoration on it."

She turned in his arms and looked at him,

enjoying the affectionate warmth in his eyes. "That's not what I meant."

She grabbed his hand before he could question her. "Let's get down the street. They'll be judging the gingerbread soon."

"Poor Shelby."

Tara laughed. "Poor Shelby my foot. She tortured us!"

"And for her to act like that, it must mean a lot to her."

"It does. Our grandmother entered every year, and Shelby likes keeping the tradition even if she's terrible at it. It's honestly the one thing she doesn't do brilliantly."

Marley caught up with them then, out of breath and still carrying her clarinet. "Can I have the car keys? I want to put this away and take off my jacket."

"I'll carry it for you. It'll take an hour for you to get through the crowd and back."

Marley unbuttoned her band jacket, revealing a loose fitting turtleneck sweater covered in sequins. She draped it over Justin's outstretched arm after handing him the clarinet case.

"I swear I've become a pack mule since that girl came to live with me," he grumbled as Marley adjusted her skirt.

"Don't act like you don't love being useful, even as a coatrack. We can store that stuff at Lady's. She has a huge table of food set up for us in the break room and wine and cider for the customers."

They made their way to the front of the

coffee shop where the gingerbread creations were displayed. Charlotte and Brandon were already there, standing with Shelby who, in her form-fitting black dress draped in tinsel and bows, stood out as a classy alternative to the tackiness surrounding them. She smiled happily and confidently even though her castle was barely standing. Tara admired the hell out of her and would love her even more after the holidays.

Brandon spotted them first and gave a brief nod. "Hey, runt. You sounded great up there. Too bad your brother didn't notice."

"Yeah, I know. He was too busy making out with your cousin."

"You just can't allow some people out in public."

Marley nodded. "Truth."

Tara couldn't help but laugh, though she could tell Justin was embarrassed by the teasing. Marley had certainly found a kindred spirit in Brandon. God help them.

Justin recovered enough to notice Brandon's sweater. "Is that a reindeer butt?"

"Yeah. It had silver bells hanging down, but Shelby said they were vulgar and clipped them."

Charlotte shook her head. "You should have known better. No way were you getting away with jingling testicles at Christmas."

Tara groaned and put her head on Justin's shoulder. "I'm sorry. Your sister is going to pick up so many bad habits from my family."

He wrapped his arm around her shoulders

and kissed her soundly, bringing about disgusted moans from the trio in front of them.

"Don't worry about it, sweetheart. The trade off is worth it."

Chapter Twenty-Two

The inside of Tara's home was as classy and elegant as the outside was hideous. All remains of the gingerbread disaster had been cleared away, and the little cottage was decorated beautifully with clear lights and garland. The tree reached almost to the ceiling and was the perfect example of Shelby's Christmas—*magic*. Justin was there for movie night, a tradition long held by the sisters and occasionally Brandon, when he could stomach it. Justin was the first outsider to have ever been included.

Justin had reluctantly allowed Marley to spend the night with her friend Molly. After much pleading from his sister, speaking with the girl's mother, and getting a more complete run down on the family history from Tara, he had let her go. The pride in Tara's eyes when he told her about it settled him, even if he had texted Marley twice already to make sure she was okay.

"Here, you're going to need this." Brandon handed him a lowball glass half-filled with bourbon.

"To watch Christmas movies?"

"Yes. We're not talking Rudolph here, man. We'll be watching made for TV chick flicks, sappy, sugar coated, and thoroughly unrealistic. Getting hammered is the only way to survive it."

"If you hate it, why do you come?"

Justin watched the path that Brandon's eyes made toward Charlotte. He looked away and shrugged. "The food's always good."

That might not have been the whole truth, but Brandon certainly wasn't lying. The food was excellent. Justin finished his drink in one gulp, earning an appreciative look from Brandon, and walked toward the food table. The girls had knocked themselves out for what Tara had described as a casual movie night. There were two kinds of soups, a plethora of dainty sandwiches, bacon-wrapped sausages, a cheese tray, and a Christmas tree made from sugar cookies. He would definitely be in a food coma when the night was over.

"If you are trying to decide what to choose, I recommend the sausage and tortellini soup. It was slaved over by loving hands for hours just for your enjoyment."

He turned around and pulled Tara close, enjoying the feel of her delicious figure pressed against him. He figured he must have looked like some sort of bug-eyed cartoon character when he saw her as he entered the house earlier that evening. Tara was the most edible thing there. Her skirt was short, her sweater tight, and the lighted reindeer antler headband nearly sent him over the edge. She was the perfect combination of class, sex appeal, and irreverence wrapped in one tight little package, and if he didn't unwrap it soon, he might start hemorrhaging.

"One of these days, we're going to have a date that doesn't involve any of our sisters."

"What a good idea."

He kissed her then, deeply, and the warmth that rose inside him had nothing to do with the bourbon. If not for the voices in the other room, he would have had her pressed against the wall.

"You taste like red wine."

"I've had a glass or two."

"Getting wasted, sweetheart?"

Tara shrugged. "It's tradition. Let's get our food. I saved us the best seats in the house."

They filled their bowls and plates, and Justin followed her back into the living room, where he saw that an oversized chair by the windows had been turned toward the TV with a tray table sitting beside it, wine bottle and glasses perched on top.

Tara set down her food and then, instead of settling on the chair, sat on the floor in front of it and pulled a blanket into her lap. Justin settled in beside her.

"Comfy?"

He pulled her legs across his and threw the blanket over them. "I am now."

She leaned in close enough for him to feel her breath on his neck. "This might make eating difficult."

His voice dropped low, mimicking hers as he ran a hand under the blanket from the top of her ankle boot, to the bottom of her skirt, and back again. "But it makes touching so much easier."

Shelby entered the living room then, looking at her watch. It was a much-needed reminder for Justin that they were not alone.

"Okay, everybody, we're going to start in five minutes. I recorded the movies, so we can skip the commercials. Everybody remember the rules?"

"There are rules to movie watching?"

Shelby placed her hands on her hips, and Justin began to fear the return of the Christmas witch. "Tara, you didn't explain everything to him?"

Tara leaned over and grabbed a glass from the table. "Sorry, sister dear. I was too busy kissing him in the kitchen to go over the schedule."

Shelby rolled her eyes and sat down on the sofa. "We'll go ahead and start. Justin, I'm sure you'll get the hang of things."

"The hang of things," as it turned out, involved Brandon making fun of the movie the whole way through, Charlotte and Shelby yelling at him for it, and a game that required taking a drink every time there was a meet cute, someone said Santa, or there was a plot point that was too ridiculous to believe. By the time the second movie started, Justin had abandoned any hope of Tara going home with him. He wanted her, but he wanted her sober.

He supposed it was for the best. If she was ready to take that step, she likely would not have drunk so much. He swallowed his disappointment and enjoyed having her relaxed form lying comfortably in his lap, though he did have to adjust her every now and then for the sake of his own sanity.

Tara looked up at him, her eyes shiny with the reflection of the lights through the window, and his chest filled with so much tenderness there was no room left for disappointment. He kissed her head and settled her back against him as her family's cajoling laughter surrounded them. He was a patient man, and everything would come in its own time.

* * *

Tara walked into Shelby's room just as she was coming out of the bathroom. Since the house was technically Shelby's and Tara and Charlotte rented from her, she got the private bathroom while the other two shared. Shelby spotted her and gasped in surprise.

"Tara, you scared me to death. What are you doing here? The way you two were carrying on, I expected you to go home with Justin tonight."

Tara flopped onto the bed, and Shelby sat beside her. "He's too much of a gentleman to take advantage of a drunk girl."

"Why would you dress like that, flirt like crazy, and then drink too much to do anything about it?"

Tara shrugged, feeling tears come to her eyes. "I thought I was ready."

"Oh, sweetie. What's wrong?"

"I think I finally understand why Charlotte gets so freaked out when she has spent too much time with Brandon. When you see forever in a man's eyes, it can be a scary thing if you don't have your shit together."

"Oh, Tara." She stroked her hair tenderly. "Really? Sounds like you need to figure out how to do that, honey. Forever is a pretty precious thing."

Tara shook her head and sat up, crossing her legs underneath her. "You know, I never thought of myself as a hot mess. But some random guy comes to town and reflects everything that's wrong with me."

"How does he reflect you?"

"He has his own issues with his parents. Even he, wonderful as he is, has baggage."

Shelby laughed softly. "You show me someone who says they don't have baggage and I'll tell you they are as real as my gingerbread men."

"He's dealing with his. And lately, I've been dealing with mine. It's still scary, though. What if it goes away or he changes his mind?"

"Stop projecting Michael onto Justin. They are obviously two different men. All you have to do is look at him with Marley to see that. His commitment to that girl is pretty swoon worthy."

Tara nodded and wiped her cheeks with her sleeve. "So, where's your baggage?"

Shelby snorted. "Oh, it's there. I just don't let it control me. I try not to, anyway. Sometimes when I see Fran, I have to fight the urge to shove her in front of a moving car, and I burn every check or gift card Michael sends. I know I should donate his gifts the way you do, but destroying them makes me feel better."

"And Justin thinks you were pretty much carved out of sugar, even after he's seen you at your worst."

"He'll learn soon enough. Are you in love with him?"

Tara quickly nodded, seeing no point in denying it. "He's the best man I've ever known. His capacity for love is massive, and he acts on it. He doesn't just spout pretty words. He has such a strong sense of justice and of doing what's right. And doing the right thing doesn't scare him. It's just part of who he is." She sighed and attempted to stem the flood of tears. "I want what he's offering so bad I can barely breathe."

"Then take it! Fran and Michael have our past, don't give them your future as well."

Tara looked at her sister for a long time. "Did they ever love us, Shelby?"

"I think so. I mean, they must have, at least some. They just loved themselves more. This might be hard to hear, but you are doing the same thing. You are letting your own BS get in the way of what's important."

Tara breathed in a slow, shaky breath then released it. "Justin and Marley are important. His plans for the farm are far more important than mine ever were. I'm glad they are there."

"Love is important, Tara." Shelby brought her close for a hug. "And so are you."

Chapter Twenty-Three

Justin reached for his phone as he sat up and rubbed a hand over his sleepy eyes. 8:00 a.m. Too early for someone to be knocking on the door. He blinked hard and shook his head, attempting to focus. He'd had a couple of drinks the night before, but that wasn't causing the fog in his brain. He was still drugged out on Tara, the taste of her mouth and the feel of her soft skin beneath his fingers. He'd had trouble sleeping, and when he finally did, it was interrupted with a restless mix of heated desire and worry that she would never be ready to take that step.

He would chastise himself for his impatience, but in the short time he had lived in Sylvan Hills, Tara had become an important part of his life. He was thunderstruck the first time he saw her, and it had only grown from there. Coming home to an empty house the night before, he realized that no matter what renovations he made, it would never be complete without her there with them.

Another knock sounded, finally breaking the fog. Thinking Marley must have come home early from her sleepover, he quickly rose, pulled on a shirt, and padded barefoot to the front of the house, opening the door without preamble. It wasn't Marley, but Tara, standing there fresh faced and smiling shyly. For a moment, right before the winter wind blew through his thin pajama pants, he thought he must be dreaming.

"Hi."

"Hi. I woke you. I'm sorry."

"Don't be. Come in."

He stepped back to allow her through, but she didn't accept the invitation. Instead, she looked at him hesitantly.

"Here." She handed a covered plate over. "Shelby made muffins."

The bottom of the plate was warm. "She was up so early making muffins? Does she bake to ease a hangover?"

Tara smiled. "No. We didn't sleep last night."

"Watching more movies?"

"Talking, mostly." She still didn't come in, but she did place her bag inside the door. "Would you mind if I walked around for a little while?"

"Of course not. Do you want me to come with you?"

She smiled. "Next time."

He cupped her cheek, leaned down, and kissed her. "I'll get coffee going. Be careful. It's slippery in some places."

Justin watched her walk away and reluctantly closed the door. She had finally come, to the door, anyway. Hopefully she *would* come inside, but even if this was just the first step, that was okay. He busied himself with coffee and then building the fire in the living room. He did everything he could think of to make her comfortable, bringing in blankets and turning on the Christmas tree lights, but eventually he succumbed to his worry and began following her path as best he could through the windows. He lost sight of her and hurried up to Marley's room to try to find her through the view up there.

Tara's red coat was easily spotted among the graying trees of the mountain in the distance. She stood still, and he fought the urge to throw on his own coat and follow her. Space. He was slowly learning when it was needed to be given. He forced himself to go to his own room for a quick shower, hoping it would quell the simultaneous feelings of excitement about her being there and worry about her being out in the cold and the idea that she might be upset now that she was there after so long.

It didn't work, and by the time she quietly knocked on the door again, he was pacing the length of the living room.

"Hey." He pulled her in and helped her with her coat. Thankfully, it didn't look like she wanted to flee. He grabbed her cold, gloveless hands and rubbed them in his own. "Let's get you warmed up."

"Thanks. I stayed out there longer than I thought I would."

Justin led her into the living room and gestured for her to sit in front of the fire where he had arranged pillows and blankets on the thick rug. He went into the kitchen for coffee and Shelby's muffins, arranging everything on the ottoman in front of Tara before sitting behind her. Leaning against the couch, he pulled her close and rubbed her shoulders while she warmed her hands on the coffee mug.

"What were you doing out there?"

She sipped her coffee and then leaned back into him. "Letting go. It's something I should have done a long time ago. I didn't realize how much hanging on to this place, to the dream of it, was holding me back. My art came from here, but it's time for me to create something different, something even more meaningful." She set her coffee on the ottoman and turned around, looking up at him with those big, warm eyes. What he saw there made his chest swell. "Justin, I am so out of my element here. I'm twenty-nine, and I've had two serious boyfriends in my entire life, and when it ended, I was more relieved than hurt. I know what I feel, but I'm not really sure what to do about it."

He leaned in and kissed her gently while stroking the strands of her soft, dark hair. "Tara, the way you helped Marley make a home here even though it had to hurt you to see her taking over a place you loved, the way you were quick to put yourself between us and Fran, and the way you comforted me when I told you about my mother and supported me with Marley. Sweetheart, you're a natural at this. I just wish you didn't think you had to let go of something important to you in order to have it."

Tara shook her head. "My grandmother would be happy that Marley is healing here the way that Shelby and I did. It makes me happy, too. It might not be in my family, but it still belongs to people I love. I'm immensely grateful for that."

Justin exhaled, and with that long breath, pieces that had splintered and separated were back in place. He'd had his own wounds, old guilt that threatened to destroy everything he was trying to build, but now she was here— with him—and nothing in the past was more important than that.

"Tara," he whispered as he gently turned her until they were face to face. He kissed her forehead, her jaw, and then trailed down her neck and back up again. Justin felt her breath hitch, and the sigh she released as he touched her sent a pulsing heat to all the right places. His hands began to roam and she did not stop him as he explored the soft curves of her body.

"I promise, sweetheart, never to give you a reason to doubt that you are cherished." The hands that had been stroking her thighs now moved to the buttons of her frilly blouse, undoing one with each word.

"Protected."

His flattened palms caressed the soft skin of her shoulders, now glowing in the lights of the tree. Justin cupped her face and waited until her dazed gaze met his. "And loved."

His mouth found hers, moving relentlessly until they were both breathless. Justin drew back slightly and stroked her neck, giving her time to pull away if she chose to. She didn't. Tara leaned closer and whispered his name on his lips. Justin felt her small hands running through his hair as she pressed against him, matching his movements as they became deeper and more frantic. Clothing was slowly discarded and they were soon lying skin to skin, reveling in the feel of their bodies moving in time to the rapid beats of their hearts.

Justin was nearly overwhelmed, amazed at the feel of the soft body beneath him. She was his very own dark-haired Venus, full of love and now expressing all that deep passion inside her for him. This was his Tara, unlocked and open to him, and Justin wanted her to feel forever with every stroke of his body against hers. She had finally come to him and he worked her body for long minutes, giving her every pleasurable reason to stay.

Chapter Twenty-Four

"So, um, Tara is at the house. She's making dinner so we might actually eat well tonight."

Justin had picked up Marley from her friend's house, and they made a quick grocery run before beginning the drive to the farm. After much satisfying convincing, Tara agreed to stay, even though she was apprehensive about his sister's reaction to her being there.

Marley looked at him and raised her eyebrows. "Did she spend the night last night?"

"No, she didn't. But, um, it is likely she will. Sometime." He could feel himself blushing in front of a twelve-year-old girl, who looked thoroughly amused at his discomfort. He returned his eyes to the road and attempted to hide a smile. "You see, when a man and a woman care about—"

"No! God no. Just stop, okay."

Justin laughed loudly as she shuddered.

Marley looked down and toyed with the zipper of her hoodie. "My mom had boyfriends. A lot of them. I used to wonder sometimes if any of them were my father."

"Did you question that, Marley? I assure you there is no doubt that William was your father."

Justin had seen the paternity tests himself.

"I know, but those other guys were there, and he wasn't."

"You lucked out, kiddo. He was not a good man."

She was quiet for a long while before she spoke again. "Then how did you learn how to be one?"

Justin had to take a moment to bite down the emotion in his throat. "I guess it helped that I hated the guy. I could see how his actions hurt people, so I would try to do the opposite of whatever he did. My mom was an incredibly compassionate woman. She always seemed to know what people were feeling, probably because she felt things so deeply herself. She hated to see anybody hurting. Ultimately, I think we all have a sense of right and wrong. Our conscience speaks loudly enough, if we just listen."

She had turned to look out the window, but Justin could tell she was listening.

"I like Tara. You unclench some when she's around."

Justin laughed again, enjoying this more relaxed version of his sister. Unclenching had its benefits. "She's nervous about how you'll react to her being there."

Marley looked surprised, which relieved Justin. He had not thought there was any need for concern, but Tara had been so nervous that he began to wonder if he'd missed something.

"So I shouldn't tease her?"

"No, go ahead. She should know what she's getting into right away. Besides, she's used to a couple of hard-assed sisters. What's one more?"

"I'll be extra nice, anyway. Just in case."

Justin realized that Marley wanted this as badly as he did. She'd lost so much. Of course she was worried she would lose this, too. They were so much alike, his two girls. Tara was probably feeling the same thing.

"I will be, too. Just in case."

* * *

"What are you so nervous about? You've had dinner with them before."

Tara held the phone to her ear as she stirred the sauce she had thickening on the stove. Justin didn't have much in his fridge that could be thrown together for a meal, but Shelby had been pleased to hear they were getting real macaroni and cheese that night.

"Yes, but it's different now. They are finally learning to be comfortable with each other. She might resent me coming in and taking his attention."

"That's a possibility. But this thing with you and Justin has been brewing for a while now. She's probably expecting it. If there are any problems, you'll work through them, unlike our sister, who is currently making a lot of noise pacing in her room."

"What's going on?"

"I don't know, but I caught Brandon trying to sneak out of here this morning."

"What? His truck wasn't there when I left."

"He parked down the hill last night to give Justin room in the driveway, remember?"

"Right. They couldn't have done anything. We would have heard them. What did Brandon say when you saw him?"

"Nothing. He just grabbed a muffin and left."

"That sounds about right. Has Charlotte been out of her room?"

"No, but I can hear her in there."

"Ugh. Can we just stay out of this?"

"I don't plan on mentioning it unless they do."

"Good plan. I can hear them pulling up. Wish me luck."

"All right. Talk to you later."

She put her phone on the counter and drew a deep breath as she heard Justin and Marley come through the back door. A second later, he saw her. Shifting grocery bags out of one hand, he pulled her close with the other, giving her a sound kiss just as Marley came into the room. Tara quickly pushed him away and then shot him an annoyed look as he laughed softly.

"Hi, Tara." Marley's chipper voice was surprising as was the quick hug she gave Tara before she set her bag on the table. "Molly's mom had a bunch of craft stuff, and we watched movies while we made ornaments. Wanna see?"

"Um, yeah." She cast a quizzical look to Justin, who just shrugged his shoulders as he put away the groceries. She looked back to the table as Marley unloaded her creations. She had mostly done sequined balls and stars, which would pick up the lights when hung in the tree. "These are nice, Marley. They are really going to sparkle in the tree."

The girl's smile seemed a little more genuine as she picked up the ornaments. "I'm going to find places to hang them."

Justin came up behind her as they watched Marley disappear into the living room. "She's nervous, too. I find it funny that I'm the only one relaxed in this situation."

She turned around to look at him. "Why is she nervous?"

"Because she wants you to stick around. Unclench already. You're making the kid crazy."

She slapped him on the arm. He picked her up by the waist and kissed her in a way that would ensure she was not only relaxed, but completely melted.

"Right. Okay, I'll stop. I should be making sure Marley is comfortable, not crazy."

"God, you're brilliant. It took the better part of a year for me to figure that out."

"Justin! When are you going to move these boxes? They are ruining the effect of the decorations." Marley's annoyed voice sounded from the living room.

"You'd think the exposed studs and patched-up drywall would be what she complains about, but no, it's two old boxes tucked away in a corner that's killing Christmas."

Tara laughed and gave him a quick hug before returning her attention to the stove. She made fast work of assembling the mac and cheese and put it in the oven before returning to his arms. He leaned against the table and held her close.

"You're so warm. I don't remember the house being this drafty when I was a kid."

"I've got to replace the windows. I'm worried what we'll find when we take out the old ones, so it will have to wait until spring. You'll have to stay with me every night, just to be sure I don't freeze to death."

Tara certainly wasn't cold after that thought. "I suppose I could make the sacrifice. I wouldn't want your frozen corpse on my conscience. We'd better get out there. I have a little experience with a sister who wants everything to be perfect at Christmas. I'll help you move the boxes and save the holiday."

Keeping one arm around her waist, he led her out of the kitchen. "I knew you'd come in handy."

When they entered the living room, they

found Marley peeking into one of the boxes. She looked up guiltily.

"What? The previous owners obviously don't want this stuff. We can at least see what we're throwing out."

Justin tisked. "Bossy *and* nosey."

Marley stuck out her tongue at her brother before pulling things from the deteriorating cardboard box.

"Looks like old Christmas decorations. Cool! I think this is part of a nativity."

Marley turned to show them a worn, nicked-up, brown stable with dried moss glued to the roof. Tara gasped and walked to Marley, gently taking the piece from her hands. She looked at it a moment and then peered into the open box.

"Where did you find this?"

Justin came to her side and put his hand on her back. "The boxes were in the attic when we moved in along with an old easel that pretty much fell apart when I picked it up."

Tara's voice cracked. "These are my grandmother's."

Sitting on her knees, she emptied both boxes, and soon, she was surrounded by memories. Justin and Marley joined her on the floor as she reverently touched each item. Some were beautiful glass pieces that had miraculously survived being stored all those years, and some were simple crafts that had been made in school. In Tara's eyes, every single one of them was priceless.

"So they weren't thrown out with everything else." Marley seemed fascinated by some of the pieces, especially the yellowed crocheted hearts and bells. Perhaps they could wash and re-starch them.

Tara shook her head. "Fran must have forgotten about them."

A few weeks ago, those words would have been spoken with enough bitterness to scorch the Christmas tree, but now it was just a matter of fact. Tara was too happy in the moment to think about the resentments of the past. She smiled as tears gathered in her eyes.

"Look." She showed a wiseman to Marley before assembling the nativity in front of them. "My gram's father carved these for her when she was a little girl. They were originally bare, but I painted them for her one year."

Justin kissed her temple. "It's lovely. You weren't the only artist in the family."

"We should put this on the mantle." Marley jumped up and grabbed a few of the pieces but then stopped abruptly. "Oh, if you want to. You probably want to take all this home, though."

Tara smiled, appreciating the girl's enthusiasm and thoughtfulness. "I'll take some home for Shelby. There are a lot of ornaments here that she made. But I'll put mine up here if that's okay."

Justin rose from the floor and pulled Tara up with him. He cupped her face in his hands, his eyes showing all the love he had expressed earlier. "It's more than okay, sweetheart. Now the tree will be perfect."

His thumbs trailed over her cheeks, wiping her tears. Tara suddenly heard music and turned to see that Marley had plugged her phone into a speaker and was playing Christmas carols.

"There. Now we're ready to decorate."

Tara could not have envisioned anything more perfect than this, not even in all her previous plans. The three of them worked together to intertwine Tara's ornaments with the ones Marley had made. The last one Tara picked up, her own clay rendering of the farmhouse, was placed on a branch next to Marley's.

Justin wrapped his arms around her waist. "I told you it would be perfect."

Marley agreed. "My mother was very particular about how the apartment was decorated for Christmas. Everything was color coordinated and perfectly placed. It was really pretty, but I like this better."

"Me too, kiddo. Feels like home."

They stood there for a long while before the smells coming from the kitchen reminded them it was time to eat. Justin asked Marley to set the table as he poured drinks and Tara pulled the dish out of the oven.

"After we finish whatever smells so delicious, I get to pick a movie."

"Something Christmasy," Tara and Marley managed at the same time.

Though she expected him to balk at the idea

after having been so inundated with the season the last couple of weeks, he just smiled as he sat down.

"Of course. Whatever makes my girls happy."

Marley smiled in satisfaction, and Tara sighed, happy to be included in his little world. They laughed their way through dinner as Tara told them about life of the farm when she was young. By the end of the meal, Marley had convinced Justin to buy goats and chickens when the weather was warmer, though he wasn't crazy about all of Marley's plans.

"I still think the idea of bathing with goat's milk is gross."

"Women have bathed in milk for centuries. It's the enzymes or something that make the skin healthy. Besides, it's going to be processed. It's not like I'm going to go out in the morning, milk a goat, and then throw it the tub."

Tara laughed as Justin just rolled his eyes and walked toward the living room. "Whatever, it's still gross. Who wants to watch a kid shoot his eye out?"

Marley followed him, petitioning for something newer, and Tara turned to finish putting away the last of the dishes. Being in the kitchen again felt new and familiar at the same time. It no longer hurt that the farm wasn't hers. She only felt joy that now it was Marley's and gratitude that she could share in it.

Tara stepped into the living room but did not join them at the couch. Instead, she went to find her bag, which she had put her sketching pad and pencils in before she left home. Tara had thought that she would do some drawing as she looked around the land, expecting every view to feel different this time.

She still wanted to capture the new energy that Justin and Marley brought to the farm but like the kitchen, those visages would be familiar even in their newness. Instead, she took her supplies into the living room and adjusted a chair to an angle where she could see the tree as well as the two happy occupants, who were currently bickering over movie choices. With a heart full of joy and wonder, Tara settled in and began to sketch from different view.

Read about Charlotte and Brandon
in *Charlotte's Landing*,
Book Two of the Sylvan Hills Series.

Coming in 2019.

About the Author

Alexis Lynne splits her time between two worlds--modern day North Carolina and Regency England. Already established in historical romance as Pamela Lynne, Alexis debuts her first contemporary work this fall. She is a happily married mother of five and resides in the beautiful green hills of Middle Tennessee. You can connect with Alexis on her Newness and Wonder Facebook page and on her website, www.alexislynnebooks.com.

For more information on the historical romance works of Pamela Lynne, check out www.pamelalynnewrites.com and connect with her on Twitter at @pamelalynne1.